SHAME

Love, Lies & Lust

A Short Story Series

By

L.L. Walton

SHAME

LOVE, LIES, & LUST

COPYRIGHT © 2016 BY L.L. WALTON

This is a work of fiction. Names, characters, businesses, places, events and incidents are either the products of the author's imagination or used in a fictitious manner. Any resemblance to actual persons, living or dead, or actual events is purely coincidental.

DEDICATION & ACKNOWLEDGEMENTS

I would like to thank my daughters, Imani and MiKayla, who have been the most inspirational and supportive of my journey. I see me in both of you. I love you to the moon and back. Jimmy Kitamirike for all your love and encouragement. Your belief in me allowed me to create miracles in my life. Thank you for being the fire under my wings.

This is dedicated to all the lovers out there. The lovers who are with their life mate, soul mate or just mate. To all my personal relationships that have crossed my path in the past, present and future, you have been my greatest influence. We are all living out our stories, be the best at your life.

LOVE & LIGHT
L.L. WALTON

LOVE

LOLA

Love was not on my to-do-list, but sex was. I didn't care too much when it came to the game of relationships. Either you were with the program or not. Either way, it was my way or no way. Men have no power when it comes to what women have and use. A man's needs are quite simplistic, and every now and then I obliged him with a little ego stroke here and a little compliment there, topped off with the greatest sex he ever had. I made sure I became what he needed and it was my goal to keep him coming back for more.

I was in love once, but it was all taken away tragically when the love of my life was killed. It left me a single mom and more alone than ever. I lost the father of my child and my best friend. The only real thing in my life. No matter what, he had my back and we had each other. It was the kind of fire in a relationship that didn't paper to justify. It allowed us to be best friends and great parents to our only daughter. Whether we were together or not, if he was alive, I could not possibly love another. Whatever me or our daughter needed, he would drop the earth to get it for us. There was an unspoken, undying love that could not logically be explained. It was the kind of love that had us in unwritten matrimony because we just loved each other. There was not anything anyone could tell us about our love. He was mine forever and even in his death, I am finding it hard to love again.

Maybe there is someone who could break this wall around my heart. This barrier that I have created to protect me from all the foolishness that goes with being in love with the wrong person. How do you move on and start to love again? I wanted to know, but until I find out, I am screwing. When it comes to spending that kind of time with a man, those are the moments I looked forward to. I didn't care about your education, job, dreams or aspirations, I wanted to be laid to sleep. And that was that. Please don't stick around for breakfast, because I don't cook to impress. If I cook for you, I just might like you. I throw down when I am in love. There's nothing greater than cooking for the man you love, everything just taste better. When he starts to catch feelings and the feelings are not mutual, it's time for me to move on. Men tend to mess up a great thing when they start to talk about being together. Especially if we began with sex. I can't take you serious. I had to control my emotions. Nothing would ever be taken from me again. If I never claimed you in the first place, then you were never mine. My heart had been broken, so I was breaking hearts and not looking back.

It had been four years since the death of Jeremy. He had died a week before my birthday, so I could never forget. I used to get so angry, so many questions left unanswered. My daughter had been my strength, she handled it a lot better than any fourteen-year-old could. She loved her father and he loved her. They looked just like and she was so much like him. He often wondered how he would handle the female version of him.

It was fun to watch. Watching them converse and spend time together. I loved those moments, I cherished those moments. Now that she is eighteen, I know he's watching in amazement at the woman she is becoming. Watching over her and smiling at the beautiful woman she has become. I love my daughter and I am very proud of her. She could have chosen to go down the wrong road, but I am glad she chooses to do what is right. She stayed close to me and made decisions to not become an out of control teenager. Things that could have been unhealthy and not good for her soul. Looking at her, I see him and that to me is the blessing.

My daughter often encouraged me to get out and date. I was dating alright; she did not know how much of a man-eater her mom had become. When she often suggested that I go online or be more social, I just smiled. I knew that one day I would meet a nice guy that would offer me a new perspective on life. He would have to have incredible patience because I do move quite slowly in matters of the heart, even if I like you right away. I was cautious with this love thing; men these days have become quite clever in concealing who they really are. I was smart enough to not get involved with a man who wasn't truly ready to be one. I took my time. I was not in a rush to be anything, but what I was and that's single. I had seen the conditions of some marriages, and it wasn't a good look. People tend to do what looks good, forgetting about the love factor. It was important to get with someone who could deal with your shit, no matter what your shit may be. For some shit, I had no patience for, not even my own.

Finding love to me was promised, as it should be to all

good women. I do not know any woman who does not want to be loved and taken care of. I knew there would be a time when love would come. I just hoped that I would be ready to acknowledge it, accept it and reciprocate all the love that is promised. My body was telling me that change was coming. I was growing bored of the dating, the self-indulgent narcissist's, and the boring conversations with men that I had no real interest in. Although I enjoyed the trips, elegant dinners and parties. The offering of dick daily becomes somewhat loathsome. My heart was ready to welcome something with more substance. Something that I could feel and enjoy and know that it would be there for the good and the bad of me. I was ready to share my life and not protect it so much from what I longed for. There was no way I could prepare for that moment until it happens. I just knew that one day it would arrive, like an unopened letter in the mail. It would be up to me to open it and explore what was inside. Once inside I would find all the things that I desired in a man. My life mate, because my soul required more than one. It would happen like a well-orchestrated song. It will fill my soul and add to my happiness and complete my greatness, because he too will have dreams to accomplish. He would be mine and I would be his and there would not be enough words to express what we would mean to each other. There would be love. The kind that kept you together for thirty plus years. There will be understanding, trust, and admiration for our differences. Two complete people coming together and becoming whole as one. That's what I want, that's what I deserve, and that is what I have coming. I know it, I feel it and I am ready.

I was getting on the BART train to San Francisco. I was running late for work and I could not even blame it on the train because it is always on time. I was frustrated that last night I had spent most of the night catching up on TV shows. I rarely watch TV, but this night required a bottle of wine and my DVR. It was also my time to relax. As soon as I laid down, I went into a coma and woke up late from the start. As I zeroed in on a seat, I bumped into what appeared to be a body. When I looked up, I was completely caught off guard by what I saw. It was a man. But not just any man, he was amazing. He was a very well dressed man, with a nice watch and shoes. His hair was low-cut with a razor-sharp beard that covered his strong jawline. He had the eyes of a warrior, very stern, yet gentle. His face sent chills down my back and left me speechless. My eyes locked in on his and I went somewhere and when I came back he was still there saying, 'Excuse me, I am sorry". How many times had he said that before I came back from my short mental trip? My cool had been tested and turned off. I felt like some little girl who was completely intimidated by a crush. I managed to say, "Oh, no problem, do you want the seat?" "Of course not", he said. "It's yours. "Do you mind if I stand here by you, this train is crowded, not much wiggle room". And then he smiled. Oh, my Gawd! His teeth were white as the driven snow and they were all his. Jackpot! Where did this man come from? How was he here in my space? I removed my eyes from his and I sat down, completely frozen. I had to regain my composure. I had to pretend like I was not moved by what just happened, so I started to do something with my cell phone, looked in my date book, trying to act preoccupied. It was like I forgot how to use my cell phone and I dropped it. Fumbled! What the fuck! He quickly picked it up, he was watching me, I could feel him watching me and it made me nervous.

"Thank you", I said. "What's your name? I thought I heard him ask what my name was, but I ignored him until he asked it again.

"What's your name?"

"Oh, um Lola, I said. As if I forgot or something.

"My name is Justin, nice to meet you". "Yes, nice to meet you too". I was cheesing way too much. Calm down, he is JUST a man! A man that has just rendered my ass helpless. I had no control over what he was doing to me and I had not even so much as touched him yet. I was feeling a bit intimidated. If he wanted my panties, I would have given them to him on the spot.

"You work in the city?" he asked.

"Yes, I work for the city in the city, yeah in the city". What the fuck was happening to my brain, why was I repeating shit? Oh, my god, he's going to think I am some idiot. "I work in the city as well; I am a lawyer". "Oh, nice. Well, this is my stop, hope you have a great day, it was nice meeting you." I ran off the train, two stops early. What the hell was my problem? I was running already. I was denying myself a chance at something and for the first time, I was afraid of what I was feeling. I left him looking confused and wanting to talk more, but I could not entertain this man. I was not as ready as I had claimed to be.

While at work, I was experiencing some kind of anxiety. I had not saw Justin on BART and I was starting to panic. Why

I was feeling so out of control, I am not sure. Maybe because I was so intimidated by this guy, I wanted him. Letting go of this control was going to be the test. I needed to let things happen. A few weeks had gone by and I was looking for Justin, but not looking for Justin. I wanted to see him, but I did not want him to see me. I wanted to act all surprised when I saw him as if I was not looking for him in the first place, see? Paranoia. I would dream of this man, like some freak. What the hell? This lack of control was killing me. But I guess this is what I needed to go through, to get to where I wanted to go with love. I had these strange feelings for someone whom I knew nothing about, how unnatural is that? I wanted to know more. I wanted to sit and talk with him and find out about him. Was he even single? Lawyer, huh? Yeah, I bet. My mind was creating every scenario possible. I had met so many pretenders, promoters, name-dropping ass, down on my luck, going through something, baby mama drama, no job having, a felon on work furlough, can I borrow liars, that I had had enough. Not only had I kissed a few frogs, I had fucked them too, so maybe the universe was shining on me now.

A few days went by and I was feeling sick. I had refused calls from my regular dose of dick, so I knew something was going on. I knew that I wanted a new experience, so I had to let all that old shit go. I was giving it up to the universe and transitioning my mind, body, and spirit. I needed this. It was time. I had to create new thoughts about what I wanted in a relationship; even if Mr. Justin wasn't the one, I needed to make those changes now.

"Hello, runaway". It was him. His baritone voice was

familiar and it scared the shit out of me. Completely cleared me of any thought I had before he spoke. I managed to say, "Oh hi". I sat there afraid to make eye contact. This time he has dressed a little more casual, maybe because it was Friday, but still well dressed. I was quiet.

"You ran off last time. Were you late?

Oh, who me? No, I just had to stop somewhere first before I got to work. Why was I lying? "Well before you get away this time, can I have your number?"

My number? Which number? My home number, my cell, you want my address, social security number anything else? It's yours, just keep looking at me with those eyes. I felt so damn crazy, but it felt so good and exciting at the same time. We exchanged numbers and made plans for dinner. It was planned for next Friday after work. I would probably go insane by then from the anticipation.

Why hasn't he called me yet? It's been a few days and I wanted to talk. Ok, that was me letting my control issues rule my emotions, again! I would have broken up with him and got back together with him, without him even knowing it. What I was feeling I could not explain. I wanted him, but I also wanted to get to know him. I was curious about him. He was a beautiful man, intelligent and handsome. He could have anything from me with those brown eyes, very intriguing. I am not too fond of guys that look prettier than me; the kind that takes longer in the bathroom than me always presented a problem. Justin had a look that complimented me very well. As if we belonged together. He didn't look like I was doing him a favor by going out with him. You see those couples and you wonder how they got together, how did that happen, what was the catch? Yeah, that was not us.

He was not as tall as I like, but he was dark and handsome, the kind that always gets me in trouble. Damn, I didn't do a dick check. I usually look at a man's hands and nose for sizing him up, but I was too busy being mesmerized, so it never crossed my mind. He was very laid back, but also confident. I smelled all that in one conversation. Now, why hasn't he called me?

I woke up Saturday morning, decided to work out. I needed to put something else on my mind except Justin. The whole time I thought of him. I had these questions and no answers. I kept telling myself, *Ok, Lola, calm down, everything in moderation, and take it one step at a time.* After my work-out, I had a voicemail on my cell.

"Hello Beautiful, it's me, Justin. Call me when you get a chance." I replayed the message five more times for subliminal messages. He didn't say when to call exactly, "Call when you get a chance." Ok, did that mean now, or would that be later? I ran myself racket over a simple message. I will call him later when I get a chance. I picked up the phone to call him right back but hung up mid-ring.

I rushed home, took a shower and tried to find a comfortable place. I was almost frantic and too excited that he called me. I needed to have a glass of wine to calm down. I waited for an hour or so before I called him back. It was the longest hour ever. I wanted to talk to him, but what would I say? I was so curious about him, yet here I am with all the crazy scenarios again. I almost didn't call. You know, the "what if's" that seem to bombard our minds when we are used to the bad? What if he's a liar or married? What if he's gay and just needed a female cover up? What if he has a small dick? How would he fuck me back to happiness when I get mad at him? What if his mother does not like me, or what if he likes his mother too much? All these things played in my head because all these things I had experienced before. I was all too familiar with the idea of things not working out. But, even with all my mental distractions, I still knew that I wanted to call him. I needed to talk to him. I was willing to take a chance on the unknown. I was not going to allow experiences from the past haunt me out of my happiness. So, I called him back.

We talked for hours. His voice was deep and he listened with understanding. I am not one for blurting out all my life's experiences, but with him, I believed that I could. This was happening so naturally that I didn't even have a chance to think about it.

After getting off the phone with Justin, I was feeling like I had finally found someone that I could connect to. It was easy to talk with him. We had so much in common. Since we have plans for dinner on Friday night, it will give me a reason to shop for something nice to wear. I wanted to show him something nice to remember.

JUSTIN

My name is Justin Aurelius Jones. I am the middle child of three sons'. I lost my older brother to drugs and my younger brother to the streets, so now I am my mother's only child. I was exposed to my father here and there, but the deaths of my brothers ultimately tore us all apart. I went with my mother and my father just disappeared.

I can't say that my life has been very hard, but it has not been easy either. Dealing with grief can be a muthafucka! It will either make you stronger or break you down. The guilt of having life and God choosing you to be the survivor has its own burdens. I am not sure how I have managed. Maybe there was no other choice and I had too. I had a mother to take care of and be strong for, it was not all about me.

I had to grow up fast. I had to be a man. Even though I was not ready to be, or had a clue to what that really meant. I was forced to figure it out; my mother guided me all the way. I had always been a good kid, but death taught me the most about life. Once it ends, that's it. Another chance will not be granted. Your decision process becomes more precise; you think differently about how you are living. You take less for granted and enjoy more things with ease. I had been exposed to both sides of life. My older brother was lost; he had made the decision to not deal with his issues. He let the streets suck the life out of him. He never recovered from not knowing who he was. He was never able to handle growing up poor. He needed things and did what he could to make it look like he was doing better than he was. He just got caught up in what was expected and what was accepted. He fell for the elusive dream of material satisfaction and died from a drug overdose. I love him nonetheless. He taught me a lot about being tough, having boundaries and learning to love yourself. All the things that he could not do for himself. My younger brother thought the streets were his friend. He wanted to roll with the thugs and have the hoe's. That was what he preferred to hang around, uplift and glamourize and ultimately it cost him his life. What the streets did to my brother's is what it does to all young men who do not know or believe there is something else. You get caught up in the local notoriety. The short-term love, the feeling of belonging to something. The streets are not loyal to anyone. It's just another temporary fix to a long-term problem, and it never ends. Dead or in jail are your options, and unfortunately, it took my brother's life without him ever having to spend a day in jail.

After high school, I went straight to college. I graduated from UC Berkeley School of Law and then to Stanford for my Juris doctorate. I not only wanted to be impressive on paper, I wanted to arm myself with the laws of this land. I knew I wanted to make a difference and not be just another person talking about the ills of our society, with no real solutions. Everybody knows it starts at home, but what if there is no home, there is no guidance. What you are usually exposed to is what you become, if there are no other options, you succumb to what you know. There had to be a better way, and there is a better way and I wanted to be an example of that.

Through my years, I haven't had much luck with women. I had a three-year relationship that ended when my girlfriend slept with her Professor. It was all over the school. It was basically a relationship of convenience at least that is what she told me. I was in love with her, she was beautiful and smart. The price of being with a beautiful woman is one thing. You deal with trust, everyone wanting to screw her and people just making up shit to test the relationship. We went through all of that and won each battle. It becomes something else if she goes out and intentionally seeks to use that beauty and brains for self-serving purposes while forgetting that she is in a relationship. Our relationship ended our senior year in undergrad. Although I loved her and wanted to marry her, the comfort of the relationship was no longer there. Complacency in relationship's breeds' monotony, so I guess it was already ending before I knew it was. After her, I just dated. Some women were very attractive, some not so attractive, either way, intelligence was a very necessary component. Even though I indulged myself now and then, I never liked dingy brods or gold-diggers or women who just try to do too much to attract a man. I learned to look at other factors, like her intentions, what she valued in life, her goals and dreams. As I got older those factors became more important to me. I wanted to be able to have a conversation with her about anything that was going on in the world. She had to understand sports or at least be willing to learn. I am a provider and I plan on being that when I become a husband. If she had her own thing going on, great! But if she wanted to stay home and birth me a nation, that was cool too. But time was not on my side. As I got older, my options were to either marry a young, strikingly beautiful woman with some of those things that I required or an older lady, who was more established and just wanted a man by her side. I knew that it would take time, I knew that it was coming, I knew that I was ready. When I saw her get on the BART train, I knew it would be her.

She was very attractive; I could not keep my eyes off her. Her cocoa skin was a compliment to her dark short hair. She looked very enticing and exotic. The beauty in her eyes stole the innocence on her face. She was not skinny, but not fat either, she was right in between a firm nice in between. She looked a little annoyed but cute. With the train being so crowded, I had to figure out how I could get close to her. I felt drawn to her. She was moving fast, trying to find a seat and when one became open, I headed for that seat too. There was this moment of awkward small talk. She had the appearance of busyness, then she was gone. Just like that. I was somewhat stunned. I was talking and in mid-sentence, she said a brief goodbye and got up and left. I wanted to know more. I wanted to see her and talk to her. Where was she really going in such a rush?

I am usually a cool guy when it comes to beautiful women. I am not easily impressed, but this woman I could not get off my mind. She paid me no attention, so I had to find out who she was. Every day for almost two weeks I looked for her. I could not find her on any train at any time. I thought of ways I would approach her, things I would say, going over it in my head. I felt like some kid or a little boy with a crush. She already had me and had no idea of what I had for her.

A few weeks went by and I was almost about to give up when I saw her on the train. There she was, her back was to me and I could see the side of her face. It was her.

"Hello runaway"

"Oh, Hi, how are you?"

"I am doing well and you?

"It's Friday, what can you say, It's the weekend."

"I've been looking for you."

"Why, do I owe you money?"

I laughed at the thought. She was funny, she made me laugh. I asked for her number before she escaped. I wanted to make sure that I could contact this woman. It became my mission to make her mine. No matter what I found out about her, I would accept it and love her anyway. It would be a week before I saw her again, but I knew I would see her again and that made me excited.

I will call her in a few days just to hear her voice. It was nice and soft almost childlike, made me imagine sex with her. But sex was not all I wanted with this one. I will wait and let her decide when the time is right.

I wanted to call her. Then thought about it. I did not want to come on too strong, so I waited about five minutes, then I called. I couldn't wait. I wanted her to feel me. I wanted to get in her head. I was so attracted to this woman, I wanted to need her even though I have no idea about her. The first ring, I was hoping to hear her voice, the second ring, I wondered what I would say without sounding too corny. The third ring, damn voicemail. I managed to leave a voice mail that ended with "call me when you get a chance". Damn, what was she doing at ten a.m. on a Saturday?

I needed to put something else on my mind. I could either go to the gym or work on this new court case I was given. I had to get her off my mind. I was not very fond of too many women, but Lola definitely had my attention. I am going to take her out to a candle light dinner, and look into her eyes and talk to her. I would patiently wait for her to return my call.

I wanted to love her. Make her feel like the Queen she appeared to be. I have never felt so compelled to show a woman that I was capable of taking care of her. Loving her the right way, and not letting anyone get in the way. I am looking at the heart of a woman. What she loves, how she loves. I wanted a friend who would accept me and love me too. I had plenty to offer financially, but there were other factors that were also important to me now. I wanted a wife and maybe a child. It was time I became a man in a different way and what better way than with a woman.

JUSTIN & LOLA

When we first made love, it was magical. It was something that I never imagined. He took the time and paid attention to my needs. We took it slow, even though it felt like it was happening fast. I closed my eyes to fully embrace what was happening to our bodies. His touch melted into my skin, we exchanged souls through a kiss that seemed to last forever. Every time I was with him, he knew exactly what to do to make me feel like I was all he wanted. He became my friend, full of laughter and simple pleasures. We enjoyed each other's company. I was finally in love.

We dated for nine months before he asked me to marry him. It had been the most amazing nine months that I could remember. The seed had been planted and we both were growing in the same direction. It was the kind of love that made you feel good all the way to your soul. He was a man's man, and he hardly let me lift a finger. I honored him and appreciated all that he did for me. He made me feel like the only woman in the world. We were in sync and took care of each other, naturally without either of us asking. We had our ups and downs, there was an adjustment that had to be made because of the hope of what this could be. This was something that we would not give up on. A love that we would work on and keep. I could never be the person I was or go back to what I was dating. This is what I was waiting for and it was well worth the wait.

The first time we went to dinner, I knew he was the one and from his marriage proposal, he felt the same way too. I knew this day would come where I would see my life unfold with the love that I deserved. Time waits for no one, but it does help you to prepare for what you want, and when you're ready it happens. It has never been my ultimate goal to marry because I was very used to being in my own space. Men would come and go, mostly go, because I was a no-nonsense kind of woman and I left the games to the boys. Marriage came when I was ready and the feelings were mutual from my man. What I am most proud of is that I have lived my life the way that I wanted to as a single woman. I have lived and enjoyed the company of some the nicest and weirdest men on the planet, but it has been this one man that I have given my heart to. This one man that I will give myself fully and without any doubts. He is the only one that has truly deserved it. My experiences good or bad have led to this very moment and I would not have it any other way.

We started a new journey together. There were times when I let my insecurities get the best of me. When I became vulnerable, I had issues trusting Justin. I was fully open and had no control and it scared me. His patience was incredible. I was carrying with me a history of being lied to so much that even being with the most wonderful man could not guarantee that I would not feel insecure. I loved him, so I had to trust him with my heart. I knew he was not like the others, so I had to give him the chance to not be like the others. There was a moment in time when I was in love with a man who would look me in my eyes and tell me he loved me every day. Then he would leave the house and go be with the next woman. I was carrying his issues that he passed on to me. The lessons in love were mine to learn and I did. I also knew that not all men are the same and I would not ever let my failed relationships make me a bitter woman. I had to own up to my part in the failure of those relationships. I am grown now and have a clear understanding of what I want in a relationship, but more importantly, how to maintain one. My old way of thinking and looking at relationships had to be based on the relationship that I was presently in. This is our love, our new beginning and I will protect and nurture this love will all I have. I know Justin is the man for me, now and forever.

After that little rift with his mother, I did not think the wedding was going to happen. My record with getting along with mothers was zero. It's not as if I was rude to them or anything, but once they met me there was always this, "Why is this bougie bitch with my son" in the air. Some were very successful at chasing me off, other times I left on my own. Who wants to compete with a mother? A woman he comes from and a woman he will go back to, if you let him. Some mothers were so attached to their son that any idea of another woman coming into the picture was seen as an immediate threat. My only thoughts are this, *"Please find a man, a hobby or senior group, bingo, casino or some other pastime."* He choose me; learn to like his decision. He has been with you since birth, let him go! Some men really get defensive about their mothers as if the world began and ended with her. A man that is too into his mom and has not grown his own balls will break up with you, just to make her happy. Luckily for me, when Justin's mom got out of hand, he respectfully put her in her place. It was nothing for him to defend me to anyone, including his mom. I was marrying the man that I had only dreamed existed, the love of my life. I am thankful that I had been given another chance to love again.

I was looking at the most beautiful woman I had ever seen. Not just your normal physical beauty that would make any man fall in love, but her beauty inside was sweet, nurturing and kind. She made you want to give her the world. I have had women in my life, but nothing compares to the touch from a woman who you know has your back. A woman who can anticipate your needs because she has been paying attention to them. A friend who can talk to you about anything or just listen, that is Lola. I cannot imagine my world without her. I thought I had everything I needed in the life, but nothing compares to the love from a woman. She had become my everything. I promised myself that I would take care of her with all I have.

When it was time for Lola to meet my mother, I wanted everything to be perfect. I flew my mom in from Florida to California. She moved there once I graduated from college. Life had been dim for her. She wanted to move where she could experience the warm sun every day. Florida was the most logical place. I took them both out to dinner. What a time that was. My mother had arrived at the restaurant before us. She had been out shopping and visiting friends all day. She was drinking wine and if she could pull out a cigarette she would. My mother was a little bit hardcore, years of doing drugs and losing two of her sons had made her that way. She was a short woman, that spoke her mind and every other word was a curse word. When I asked her why she cursed so much, she said, "Because I am fuckin' honest."

"Hi ma", as I kissed her on the cheek, this is my fiancée Lola.

Lola? Hi, as she leaned back to get a full view of her. 'You pretty", where you from?"

"Hi, Miss Jones, nice to finally meet you. I was born in Mississippi, but raised in California". "So, are you a Southern Belle or California girl"? Her laugh was hearty filled with years of smoking cigarettes. I smiled. An answer from me would open up all kinds of conversation and I was not in the mood.

She sipped her wine while still looking at me. I could see where the rim of the glass and her eyes met. She was checking me out.

"What kind of work do you do Ms. Lola?

"I work for the city of San Francisco, executive assistant to the city manager."

"Oh, so what you do, get his coffee?" There was that laugh again. This time Justin interrupted, "No, ma. Lola's position is actually pretty important and goes way beyond getting coffee. She has a master's degree in public administration. That's why I am making her my wife, so I can stop working. His sarcasm went over both of our heads. There was a moment of silence, then the shit hit the fan.

"You know Justin don't keep girls around long, I am surprised he asked you to marry him on such short notice, are you pregnant?"

I sat there in silence, but the first thing that came to mind was; *No, I am not pregnant, but we do fuck enough to have triplets by now.* I knew she was trying to get under my skin and at this point, I was refusing to take the bait. This mother shit can be tricky, one wrong statement and it could ruin our relationship. I did not want to be disrespectful. I decided to let Justin handle his mother and I excused myself to the bathroom.

I looked at my mother in disbelief, she was sitting there like she had won the war.

"Look ma, Lola is going to be my wife. You are going to have to respect and accept her as your daughter-in-law. I love her and she is not like any other woman that I have ever been with. I need you to accept her. It doesn't have to be today, but at least before we bring your grandkids into the picture." My mom just looked at me with tears in her eyes. All the strength in the world could not hold back those tears. Tears that I had not seen since my brothers died. In her silence, I knew she understood what I was saying.

Here I am standing in the bathroom when I want to just walk out the door. Thank the heavens I have a man that defends me and loves me. I will have to get along with her eventually, but right now she has pissed me off and I do not have much to say. Alright, deep breaths Lola, go back in there and finish dinner.

We had our wedding at Martha's Vineyard with a few close friends. Justin looked as handsome as ever, in his egg shell colored suit. When you look out over our wedding you could see the white flowers that intertwined with the greenery. The aisle that I walked down was red and all the chairs had white and pink flowers attached to it. Pink was my daughter's idea, who also was my bridesmaid. It was a very magical moment, one that I will never forget.

RACHEL DAVENPORT

Frank could have been a woman's dream if he could just get his shit together. He worked as a consultant for a major accounting firm, and he did some work under the table. It was the work under the table that had him up at night. He had a temper that he could not control, but he loved life and I loved being with him. He never asked for much and all he wanted was to be with someone who could accept him as he is. Which was a bit much considering he had seven kids and five baby mamas'. None of which he made no attempt to marry. Those facts alone would make any woman think twice about being serious with this man. He was a fun guy that sold you a believable fantasy, topped with unbelievable sex. A control freak, he used people and once he was done, he left. It worked for five women and who knows how many others. But too bad for them, those were issues I will never have. I had no intention of having children with Frank. I married him because he has a lot of money and over time, I fell in love with him. Although I was stunned when the judge gave him 10 years in prison for laundering money, I was determined to still live my life.

Being in love with a man who is locked up is some fucked up shit. There is no way around it. You can try to live your normal life, but normal is being with him. I had a lot of time to do a lot of shit. You must deal with his insecurities and wondering what the fuck you are doing at all times of the day. Questioning you about shit you never heard of. Always wanting to know who you been talking to, where you go today? Who you go with and why? That shit alone will get on your nerves so bad, you just want to tell him, "Call me when you get out!"

I am married to Frank so all he wants to do on the congenial visits is fuck. Who wants to fuck on these hard ass bunk bed mattresses? I know the guards are either watching or listening. There is no privacy in jail, I do not care what they told you. I am not sure what I was looking for when I went to see Frank. I wanted him to be like he was when we were out and at home. But it seemed like he turned into this dictator, with no feelings or emotions. You would think he was in jail for murder. But he was in jail for a paper crime, a crime that could have been prevented if he had the right people around him. He took the fall for three other fools who should be doing the time. There is no loyalty among thieves, and Frank learned that the hard way.

During our visits, Frank never cared enough to ask about me. He just wanted to make sure the bills were paid and that his kids were taken care of. The only thing he had left to say to me was, "Let's fuck." That's all there was between us. He liked it from the back. He fucked me hard and had no compassion for me at all. He was taking out all his aggressions out on my vagina and I did not deserve that at all. A big dick doesn't feel good unless you want it. I needed to be held and kissed, then fucked. Being with him had me wanting something more. I had always been faithful to him, but I do not see myself doing this shit for another eight years and I am finding it hard to be faithful to an invisible body.

After a long day at work. I was ready to have a drink and relax for the evening. I walked to the nearest bar that I could find. There is always this unspoken vibe when a woman walks into a bar alone. She is either there to pick up a man, meet someone, or lonely. Today, I didn't give a shit about opinions, I just needed a drink. I sat at the bar, ordered a double shot of Hennessy. Yes, it was that kind of day. I started to think of my husband who was doing all this time and how I was spending mine. I wanted to feel guilty, but I didn't. I wanted to let him know that he no longer controlled my every move and that I was living out every fantasy without him. I wished he knew me better, I wished I showed him more of me. The more of me that was a lot like him. In mid-thought, I was interrupted by a deep voice, a voice that left me almost speechless.

"May I sit down?"

"Yes". As I looked over my shoulder, this man was very handsome. He had these incredible green eyes, that was surrounded by his dark mocha skin. His beard was unkept and rugged. His clothes were well put together, not the white t-shirt shit that most men that approach me have on. There isn't anything worse than seeing a forty-year-old nigga still buying white t-shirts from the local liquor store like that shit is designer. This man was nice and appealing. His lips looked like he could suck a plum out a peach. He asked me a lot of questions, some which I lied about some which I told the truth. Are you single? Yes. Are you married? No. Are you looking? Well, of course. I thought I could always use a man to play with and to take up some of my time every now and then. Are you available? The more alcohol we shared the more he opened up about the complexity of women, his life and what he wants most from the world. Things that at the moment, I didn't care about. Solve your issues before you get to me, I am not a therapist. I listened anyway, as I wondered what it would be like to sleep with him. I wondered how he used his hands or if he was a good lover or just a fucker. I wanted to know, but something was telling me to take it slow and see what happens. I already had a boy in my toy box, did I need another one?

We fucked the first night and every chance I got. There was nothing amazing about him at the moment, but his dick. Although very attractive, he wasn't anything that I would look at twice. He soon became the missing piece to an otherwise boring existence. The attraction I am not sure, our worlds would have never collided, but the convenience was that he did not require all the necessities that a normal man would. He did not have a long drawn out story about his life. I thought I would keep him around often enough for him to feel needed, but not enough for him to think that I was in love, or wanted to establish any kind of meaningful relationship. That's what I needed right now, someone who did not ask a lot of questions and who would not interrupt my everyday life.

He was completely innocent to the world that I am from. He held his own and wasn't afraid of me. He was well traveled in the U.S, but not other countries. His life was filled with a little hood, with a bad boy gone good story line. All he knew was the hood. He wanted more and was striving to create what he believes is an ideal life. He was the perfect candidate for what I had in mind. He had never even been in love. Never been to jail, and never had dreams, until now. I always thought how amazing it was how a woman could change a man's whole outlook on life, or destroy it all together. Good women made you want to do better, hood women made you want to stay the same. His purpose in my life would be to complete the task of satisfying me until my husband returned from prison; he had eight more years to go.

It was our first date. He did not have a car, so I picked him up. This normally would be a problem for me, but I wasn't in this for the long haul. I was in it for temporary satisfaction. He lived in the hood. The same hood I grew up in and moved away from. As I drove my new C-class Mercedes, all eyes were on me, thank god for tinted windows. I did not want to be seen. This time he was dressed more casual. He wasn't sagging, that's all that mattered to me. He wreaked of weed and alcohol. He was happy, loaded and in a good mood, so I decided to not take this man out in public. I took him to a hotel.

I got a nice little suite out by the embarcadero. It was by the water and created a nice ambiance. Once we were inside he looked me in my eyes and walked over to me and slowly took my clothes off. He kissed my shoulders and neck. He was tall standing in the back of me, we walked over to our reflection in the mirror. He removed his clothes and stood behind me with my breast in his hands and his hard dick touching the spine of my back. I closed my eyes and said a prayer, *"God I pray that*

I get fucked good tonight. I pray that he doesn't cum fast and talk too much during sex. I pray that in the morning, he can go his way until I need him again with no drama and without asking for any money. Amen." He continued to kiss my neck while massaging my breast. He proceeded to bend me over so that I could see myself and him in the mirror. He tried to enter without a condom, but I was not having that. I put the condom on with my mouth. He entered me softly and thank god, he had the goods. He went deep and slow, I was watching him watch me. This was intense. Not what I was expecting. He continues to give it to me deep and with each thrust he made sure I was feeling him. He was looking at me in the mirror, he didn't take his eyes off me. He grabbed my shoulders to pull me closer and to go deeper. He closed his eyes and was no longer watching me. He was giving me complete pleasure. All you could hear was the sound of our breath. He turned me around and picked me up and took me over to the bed. He placed a pillow under my ass and continued to go slow and deep, placing one leg on his shoulder, he went in deeper and harder. I was so wet; I could not control the fact that he was making me cum. He moaned as if the reward was making me cum. We made love a few more times. I was completely worn out. We laughed and talked until four in the morning. I cannot get all into my feelings, although he was pulling me in deep.

After a long night of complete satisfaction, I saw that my husband had called several times, so he had to go. "Hey Boo, he said". There is nothing more irritating than hearing a man call you boo when you have no intention of ever being his boo, so I just looked at him.

"Hey, did you have a good time last night?

"Yes", I did, did you?

"Yes, when can I see you again?"

"I am not sure"

It wasn't my normal conversation with someone I was just sleeping with, but there were a genuine concern and interest in his tone and I liked it. I was thinking about it even before I left him. I was not sure how to process this feeling, but to just bury myself in my work and forget about what was ringing in my head. As far as I was concerned I had just fucked, Idris Elba or Denzel Washington.

A few days went by and before I knew it, it was time for me to visit my husband. It was something that I dreaded and seeing him locked up didn't make it any better. I was also thinking about the stain Malachi had left. I was sore from the damage and I wanted more. I just wasn't sure what he wanted. He made no demands, didn't ask for any money and was all about pleasing me. That's something that will be hard to let go. Men these days expect you to dish it out. Some expect you to pay for drinks, dates and all kinds of shit as if they have a pussy. If I had plans to be with you, yeah maybe. If you are my man, yeah maybe. Dishing out money for a fool with no job is quite motherly and I am not trying to be anyone's mother, so I hope he has some kind of income because this mama doesn't pay for dick.

Frank wanted to see me every weekend. I could not see him every weekend. I did not want to see him every weekend. Most of the time when I did drive to Solano County to see him, we argued about me coming to see him more often.

"Why can't you see me every weekend? What are you doing on the weekends?

"I work hard during the week and I would like to just take my mind off things on the weekends."

"If I find out you been cheating on me, you and your little boyfriend are going to pay the price, so be careful, these bars are invisible to me."

I smiled and got a little closer, "You don't own me. I can do whatever I want."

"I do own you, we are married remember?"

This was going nowhere. We just sat there and talked about finances, they only thing left that we could agree upon. I was still paying people and bills. I was still taking care of his children, dropping cash here and there. He wanted to keep everyone happy, but me. He had other accounts and I found out he had another woman.

I was at the bank one day and the woman in front of me was making a withdrawal from an account with her and Frank's name on it. She said she was making a withdrawal from a Mr. and Mrs. Frank Davenport's account in the amount of ten thousand dollars. I moved a little closer to hear what was being said.

"Yes, Mrs. Dandridge, how are you today? Can I have your account number and ID?

"Sure. My husband is out of town on a building project and needs the money to pay employees. If only he would take care of things before he leaves town." She had two small children with her and based on their big ass heads and noses, they were Frank's children. There was nothing in me that would allow me to say anything. And was she calling herself Mrs.? Has he married someone else or pretended to? Frank would do anything for appearances. He would also do anything for some ass. I know damn well that he is not married to another woman!

I was next in line. I made the deposits into my account. An account that I had in my maiden name. My identification did not even have my married name. I have never changed anything I had before him and with good reason. I would wait for him to call. By that time, I would be calm and would act like nothing was wrong. I needed to drag this out, so when I ask again for my divorce, it won't be a problem.

I was back at work when I received the call. Frank wanted to know where his money was. I just listened to him scream and holler while I filed my nails.

"You bitch, if you have stolen money from me, it's your life. I am going to send someone after you and your little boyfriend, let me find out who he is." You hear me? Huh? I know you hear me, bitch! I will kill you!

"Hello?"

"Yes?"

"Don't do this shit, I mean it!

"Are you serious Frank? Are you threatening me while you are in jail"?

After about five minutes of listening to his bullshit. I said, "I saw some woman at the bank with two of your kids taking ten thousand dollars out the bank." Now tell me why are you bothering me? I want a divorce. I want it done quietly and professionally. And then I hung up.

MALACHI

Ms. Rachel Davenport, a high-class woman with exotic sexual needs. To put it simply, she was a super freak. I had to step to her when I saw her at the bar. She must have thought that I was some wiener, but I am going in for the kill. I am going to make her mine. I am going to play by her rules for now, but soon she will be mine. I have plans for Ms. Davenport. The way she was giving it up made me think that no one was giving it to her right, if at all. I will be that man. We may not be in the same league, but I have something she needs. She wants to be loved and given some attention and I am the man for the job. She may come off a little tough, but she makes love like she longs to just be treated like a woman. A woman that could use some taking care of.

I used to run through women, but now I want something more. I have not had the best life, but it is my life and the choices I have made have led me to this. There are so many women who would pay for love. You would not believe the things a woman would do just to have a man. The problem I am having is, if it's too easy, I don't want it.

Through the eyes of some, I am not rich. I don't look rich and I surely don't act rich, but I can take care of a woman. Rachel is really a dope ass women. Educated, fine and got her shit together. Some men are intimidated by that, but it draws me in. I like a sharp woman, turns me on. Now that we have made a connection I feel that I have a chance. I don't know much about her. She didn't want me to know anything. I didn't ask too many questions, I wanted her to enjoy herself. But I was able to give her what she has been missing and that's some long and strong love. We talked about shit that I do not normally talk about with women I am not serious about. She was different, not a push over. She seemed like the type that could take this good dick and not look back, so I took a chance. I will call her in a few days.

She called me the next day.

"Hello?"

"Hi Malachi, it's me Rach, what you doin'?"

"I am just relaxing at the moment, what's up?"

"Just saying hello"

A few hours later we were both back at the hotel ripping each other apart. What I was capable of was no longer a secret. She took it like a pro and gave as much as she took. Rachel made sure that I knew she was the boss. She had all the control, she made me cum this time and I was caught off guard. She was a gentle beast in bed and I loved it. I know this is not the normal way to start a relationship, but I was all in. I was not letting this pass me by.

Six months later and time after time after time, I was hooked and so was she. This love making was so intense, I guess it was what we both needed. We not only enjoyed each other sexually, we were able to connect in many other ways. We spent a lot of time just talking. She was able to open me up and ways I hve never experienced. When I am with her, I feel like I can do anything. This could be dangerous because I was willing to kill to keep her in my life.

We were talking one night and she told me she was married. She said her husband was doing at least ten years and was two years in. I was shocked to hear that she was married, but I wasn't surprised. She was the type to be married or taken. I wasn't sure how to feel. I felt that she allowed me to walk into something and I wasn't given a choice in the matter. For the last six months, I have been sleeping and falling in love with a married woman. No wonder she was at the bar drinking. I could not process how a woman so intelligent and beautiful could be involved with a fool in jail. How did this shit happen? She told me her husband was an accountant and laundered millions, and some of his friends had snitched. He will be in protective custody when he comes home and she was not sure about the state of their marriage. I wanted to tell her to, divorce that mutha fucker! But I put my kind and understanding face on and hoped that she did not think that I was just going to disappear. I am going to make sure she gets a divorce. I felt it was my duty. Rachel had no idea about my other life as a hit man. I was trying to change, but life sometimes calls you to be things that you would not normally be. Things you would like to leave behind or to erase. I was no longer in the streets, but the "go to" man if all else fails. My past was just that, my past. It was time I let that hood life go. I was able to stash severl thousands in my storage. If I have to get rid of her husband, then I will. At the moment he does not seem like a threat, but once I am ready to marry her, I wanted to be able to. I am going to lay back and let her decide how she wants to do this, but it would be nothing to get rid of him.

I let go of the women I was messing around with. There was no way I was going to let anyone interfere with this relationship. I was falling in love, feeling things that I never have. I really enjoyed just being around her. I was calm when she was near. I could just stare at her for hours and enjoy every moment. We cooked together, shopped, took small trips and loved on each other every chance we got. This felt like a real relationship, something I had never had. The world meant nothing as long as she was with me. She gave me a new look on life and I wasn't looking back. I don't even believe I have never told a woman I loved her outside of my mother. I loved Rachel, one day I will tell her. That's just how incredible she was. There was nothing on the planet that would make me stop seeing her, not even her husband. He fucked up and I was glad he did. Rachel and I are no mistake. If this fool in jail becomes a problem, he may never see me, but he will feel me.

I could hear her on the phone talking to her husband. The conversation seemed long and boring. She was asking him to do something, I could not completely hear what it was. She was pleading with him and I didn't like it. Let me just get rid of this fool. I didn't like to hear her upset especially if there was nothing I could do about it. When she returned to the living room she had tears in her eyes.

"Baby, what is it?

"He's not going to give me a divorce, she said. Her voice was trembling and she looked hopeless. It was a different Rachel. She was crying and that shit pissed me off. I have never seen a woman I cared about cry. It wasn't a cool feeling. All she had to do was give me the word and I would make it all disappear. I could get anyone touched in or out of jail. I wanted to show her that I could take care of anything, but it wasn't the right time.

RACHEL & MALACHI

I had never contemplated divorce until I started sleeping with Malachi. There were a lot of things that I was contemplating. Here I was in love with a man with a high school education. He is definitely not my idea of what I thought "the one" would look like. Frank was more of a financial fit; a certificate with nicely scribed words on a paper that didn't mean anything to either of us. But we tried anyway. There was no butterflies or love at first sight kind of moment. We just hooked up and got married. On the outside, we are the perfect match. I am young and ambitious, he's older and well-seasoned. We were an attractive couple; I guess no one had to know that we didn't have shit in common.

I know that my friends and family would want me to get my head checked if they met Malachi. This was supposed to be a fling until my hubby came home or until one of us tapped out. But now I am in love with him. He had come into my life like a cool breeze. His attentiveness, love and time had me in a place of confusion. What would I tell my husband? Could I tell my husband? I had eight more years to decide. I was determined to enjoy my life with Malachi. He made me feel things I did not feel with my husband. The decision has been made, I wanted him in my life.

Malachi protected me and had my best interest. He was not able to compare financially, but he did the best he could. He bought me nice things, but I never questioned where the money was coming from. It was not my concern. He was a handyman around the house, we talked about a lot of things. I was impressed, he was smarter than he looked. He worked, paid attention to my needs and we have connected so deep sexually that it seems spiritual. What else could a woman ask for? There was an incident with some random chick who thought she could just walk up and sit on my man's lap. She got corrected, he handled it like a man and sent that chicken on her way. A simple man would have been stuttering trying to figure out what to do or say, but he did not play. There will be no disrespect in his presence.

I wrote my husband a letter asking him for a divorce. I did not hear from him for a few weeks, no phone calls, nothing. Then out of nowhere, I received a letter. He was livid! He threatened my life and promised to ruin my life if I moved on with someone else. I expected that. He meant everything he said. I married him for financial reasons, but I did not love him like a wife should. We both knew that. We made money together. But that money was not keeping me warm at night. That money was not making love to me or keeping me company. Deep inside I wanted more. When Malachi came into my life he gave me exactly what I needed. When I needed it. It became more than just sex. We connected on every level. He became my friend, someone I could trust and run to, I just can't let him go.

I told Malachi that my husband was not willing to give me a divorce. He just told me to give it time, things were going to change real soon. Frank held to this marriage as long as he could. One day I got the call that he was found dead in his jail cell. He had been stabbed over a hundred times. I was devastated at the violence, but relieved that the fight between us was over. He had a two-million-dollar life insurance policy that was paid out to me. I gave all of Frank's children a fair share. I really did not want to hear from any of them again. I was able to be with Malachi fully and completely. I no longer looked for temporary satisfaction. I was living a dream with the love of my life.

That same year, I became pregnant. For the first time, I was going to be a mom. I could not have been happier. Malachi had more than proved that he was father and husband worthy. We packed our things and moved to Washington. It was a place where neither of us knew anyone and we both deserved this fresh start. When I think back to how I just wanted someone to sleep with, Malachi made me realize how much I was missing from a loving relationship.

SUGAR BELLE

My name is Sugar Belle Lane and I am in love with a drug addict. His drug of choice is cocaine, mine is him. Under any other circumstance, we probably would have never met, but social media gives you access to people, places and things and you would have never known. Someone could pop-up on your timeline, make a comment, or "like" something you say and that could be all the attention that is needed to start a relationship

When I was young, we were a family, who went to church every Sunday, Wednesday and Saturday for choir rehearsal. My real name is Sugar Belle, so when the choir director asked me what my real name was, I wasn't sure what she meant. She called me everything but my name, Betty, Sugar, Bella, Shanna and the list goes on. It annoyed me heavily to hear my name mispronounced for so many years. I really thought this woman was deaf, so after a few times correcting her, I gave up. She didn't want to pronounce it right. If you don't get if after three years, then you didn't want to get it.

Sunday's were filled with the usual stuff. Sunday school, service, dinner and back to church to get the rest of what God didn't give you during the last few services. It was always fascinating to watch Sister Goodman jump all over the church like she was running hurdles. Every Sunday at about a quarter after one, Brother Carter would start speaking in tongues. His wife would follow shortly after, then their kids joined in, jumping all in a circle as if to do some kind of tribal family chant. They were strange, but no one said anything about it. They all must have thought it was an act of God.

After all the excitement, the beating of the tambourines, drums and organ. The church would become quiet and the tone would calm to a whisper. The preacher would get up and ask if there was anyone ready to give themselves over to God. Everyone would sit there waiting to see who would go first. For some reason, it was always the brother who wore the three-piece tangerine colored suit, who probably just came from the club, who would get in line. He would get in line with his Jerri curl soaked collar. He looked as if he had just run straight from hell into the church line. He would be sweating profusely, like he knew if he did not come and get in that line, God would surely strike him dead. If he was able to stand in that line of shame, God would surely forgive him for another week.

Going to church was tiring, but it was the only social life I had. It would also be the first place that I realized that I was a different kind of child. Life was blooming and I was changing. Church was like watching reality TV, live and you knew every character personally and everyone had their role. It was also where I would find my first forbidden love.

Most of my life I had very little interest in boys. One reason was because I was a tomboy myself. I played sports, I fought with them and ran with them. I had a few friends that were girls, but they were only good for sleepovers. Then there was David. David was a singer in the church choir. He was tall and somewhat of a mystery. He had several brothers and sisters. He was the oldest of his siblings and that was the only thing we may have had in common. He was also about twenty-one years old at the time and I was thirteen. I did not understand the age difference, all I know that each time he sang in church no matter what he was singing, he was singing to me. He had the most beautiful voice I ever heard. I now looked forward to going to church just to see him. There was no way that I could have this man call my house. He was a grown man, and that would not sit well with anyone. I had to figure out a way to see him outside of church. We would see each other in passing and at church functions, and he would give me a handshake and a kiss on the forehead. That was the most annoying thing ever. My virgin self wanted him to kiss my lips and hold me close, I guess he too knew his limitations. I wanted him to be my first, but how and when this would happen I just didn't know.

The affair with David went on for many years. He never had sex with me, but he did do other things that brought me great pleasure. We would sneak and see each other where ever he was. David went on to become a great R& B singer, with many hits. Whenever he was home, he would call and we would get together and do what we always did. That was the theme of our relationship, until one day he told me that he was in loved me. I never quite understood what that meant. I am twenty now and he is twenty-eight. By this time, I had lost my virginity, fell in love, and even experienced heartbreak. I was not ready for him to love me that way. I wanted to continue what we had done for the last six years. He cheated on girlfriends to be with me, he lied to his family because of me, and I did not want to enter a relationship with a man who I only thought of as a friend. I wanted to be in love, have a baby and have a normal life. But what was normal?

According to your parents and the bible. You went to school, college, got married, have some babies and work the same job for twenty odd years. That was so far from the program I had in mind. How boring to follow that guideline? The ultimate guideline to misery. If you did not follow it, you were looked upon as a sinner or even worse a human being. I was living like a caged bird, waiting to break free and fly. I wanted to be accepted for who I am and not for what I did or did not become. I was not going to be the one that followed the rules of society. It was always a battle between doing what's right and doing whatever.

Whenever I had sex, I felt so much guilt because I was not married. I also felt a sense of freedom. I was no longer a virgin. I had tasted the other side of the forbidden fruit and I liked it. Why must marriage be the gateway to sex? I am sure there were millions of people who have been unable to abide by the rules and regulations of how society says your life should be. How can a religion put such unrealistic expectations on people? Then make you feel low when you are unable to abide by every single rule. No human on earth has been able to abide completely by the ten commandments. That would require perfection. I also learned early on that you cannot really have a platonic friendship with a man, unless he is gay or bi-sexual. Eventually someone will want to cross that line. Whether you deny or engage, the friendship changes no matter what.

I was almost thirty years old when Damien entered my life. I had had six abortions by the time I was twenty-five, and I wanted to have a different experience. It was obvious that I was desperate for love and looking in all the wrong places. I wanted to have great sex, a loving relationship, go to work and enjoy my friends and family. My life was simple. I was dating, but not real serious about anyone. I have had a few suitor's whom I adored, but there wasn't anyone that could keep my attention. I would be bored with the suits and not entertained enough by those otherwise. When I meet Damien, he was very attentive. I loved the attention he gave me, but when it came to other things he failed. He failed over and over again. He was no longer able to hide his addiction. I started to notice him changing and started to ask questions, soon after it all came crumbling down.

Damien was slim. He was muscular and in shape. He had eye's so stern, he could see right through you. His Scorpio nature led him to be very hot-tempered and out of control. But on other days, he went to work and seemed regular. He had a kind nature and a love so deep that I could not deny it. I loved what he was and what he could be. I fell in love with the moments of laughter and insane love making. I had no doubt he was the best and I would spend the rest of my life with him. He was the type that could get me in trouble; he could be reckless and immature. But I decided to spend time with him anyway, he was adventurous and I loved that about him. I do not care who you are, if you began to spend time with a man or woman who is good or bad for you, one will rub off on the other and that could either be good or bad.

It all started very casual. We talked a lot. He called me every day and soon he moved in with me. It was perfect until I realized that he smoked cigarettes every day, he smoked weed every day and he loved cocaine. By the time I found out about his habit, he had been a cocaine user for over five years. It was not just a habit; it was a way of life. Soon, there was money missing, jewelry or anything that he thought was valuable. Here was this amazing man, whom I loved, battling demons that he was trying to keep away. Soon I did not recognize the man that I loved. We started to argue and he would disappear for hours, returning only to go to sleep. He was leaving for work every day, but never made it to work. He had lost his job months before and was pretending to have a job. Watching someone I love fight this battle was depressing. If I didn't love him, I would kick him to the curb and leave him alone, but I couldn't. When I looked into his eyes, I still saw the man that I loved, but I also saw a man fighting a battle of this life. I often would stare at him in his euphoric state, trying to find the man that I had fallen in love with, the man that made me laugh, encouraged me, believed in me and accepted my craziness. Now that I knew his secret, I had become the enemy and living together was starting to look like a bad idea.

I mentioned him trying rehab, but as far as he was concerned he had it all under control. He had lost his job, lost his car, and on the verge of losing me. Since he had not actually lost me yet, he felt that the world was good and he had no problems. The secret was out and I was still here trying to love him anyway. And I did. I knew that the Damien that I loved was still there inside, but there was nothing that I could do to bring him back. It took me a long time to realize that in order for him to get better, I needed to leave him alone and for me that was almost impossible. I wanted him to be ok, so I supported his habit. I didn't mean to support his habit, I just didn't want him to get hurt or have to rob and steal in order to get what he needed. It was terrible thing for me to do, but I loved him and I wanted him to be ok.

There is nothing more heartbreaking than watching someone battle with life and inviting drugs to join the battle. There is nothing you can do but pray. Damien came home one day and he was pacing and walking all over the place. He was sweating and talking fast, kind of mumbling and I was not sure what he was talking about. He looked as if he had not slept in days. His face was starting to sink in from days of not eating. I was not sure who he was anymore. I wanted this nightmare to stop. I was watching such a beautiful person destroy himself. Whatever he was battling, he was losing and it was starting to show.

I asked him to leave because looking at him this way was unbearable. He never really wanted to talk. He showed up and then disappeared, then slept all day. That was not the life I wanted and in order for him to change, I needed to no longer be a crutch. I eventually kicked him out and I became public enemy number one. He yelled and called me all kinds of disrespectful names. He threatened to blow my house up and kill my whole family. He was beyond angry, but I had to kick him out.

Not even twenty-four hours later he was back on the phone, begging and pleading wanting to come home and of course, I let him. He promised to not do drugs. He promised to get a job, he promised to never verbally abuse me again and to change his life. Within one week, all of those promises were sidelined for another hit. I came home from work and he was leaned over so deep, his head could have touched the floor. I tried to wake him up and he just laid there stumped over unable to move or respond, so I prayed for him and left him there.

Damien managed to wake up at three in the morning. He was making a lot of noise in the fridge, moving things around. I wanted to get up and see what he was doing, but I did not want to engage with him this early in the morning. I just laid there hoping that he would find what he was looking for. A few hours later it was time for me to get up and go to work. Damien never made it to bed. I managed to get up and see where he had fallen asleep. I walked in the living room and he was not there. I didn't hear or see him in the bathroom or any other place in the house. I decided to go downstairs to the basement. No one ever went down there, but it could be a great hide out if you wanted to get away with something.

I opened the door to the basement and I heard the TV. I walked down the stairs and there he was lying naked from the waist down with some girl sleeping over his lap. I went over to wake them up and it seemed as if they were in a coma. I went upstairs and got a bucket of water. I made sure it was real cold. I poured it on the both of them and they sprung up like a jack in the box. Damien looked shocked and I was screaming, "Who the hell is this woman in my house"? Have you lost your fucking mind? You bring some dope fiend girl in my house and you are fucking her in my basement? What the hell is wrong you?

It was clear what was wrong, he was on drugs. He was making drug moves, drug decisions and it had nothing to do with me. He got up and left with the girl and did not say a word. He just looked at me as if I was in the wrong house and left with her. I was livid, then I was hurt and then I was depressed. I later threw a complete tantrum. I through shit all over the house, broke glasses, lamps, and whatever else I could see. What part was I missing? Why am I not seeing what I needed to see? This man is absolutely no good for me. There was nothing that I could do to bring my Damien back to me. I did not understand what was happening and I was sure that I had lost him. My life would be nothing without him.

I refused to go to work. I gathered myself enough strength to make me dinner. I had been locked in the house for a few days and I wasn't feeling like getting out of bed or talking to anyone. I wanted him. I refused to call his cell phone. He called me a few times, but I was unable to answer. What could he say? What could I say? I knew that I loved him and I wanted him back in my home. I knew we could get through this and that he belonged to me. I did not care about the woman he was with, she meant nothing. She is only there because the drugs are there, he was not in his right mind.

A few weeks had passed before I heard from Damien again. He wanted to come home. He was hungry and needed clothes and food. I let him come home again. The first few weeks were very nice. He was looking for work and taking care of the house while I was at work. I was hopeful this time. I was happy that he was with me. We were making love and enjoying each other's company like the early days. My best friend was back.

Damien and I had decided to go for a walk around Lake Merritt. It was a sunny Sunday afternoon. There were plenty of people out jogging and walking. We would stop for lunch at the local sushi place and continue our walk. We were making our way past East 14th when a man ran up to Damien and asked where was his money? I was stood there while Damien explained that he would have it to him soon and he needed a few days to get the cash.

I asked Damien how much cash did he owe? He just continued to look at the man in the car.

"Damien? How much cash do you owe?"

He completely ignored me.

The guy looked at me up and down and asked Damien how much are you willing to pay?

Damien looked at me, in his eyes I saw fear and confusion. He asked me if I was willing to pay his debt and of course I would. Then he started to look at me funny and said, 'He doesn't want money, he wants you."

Me? I said. He wants me? He wants me to do what?

Damien walked me over to the curb to talk in private.

"Look, Sugar Belle, he wants to sleep with you and he will completely forgive my debt. I won't owe him nothing. Just this once, and I promise never to do drugs again." The tears swelled up in my eyes at the thought of my man asking me to pay a debt with my body. He actually wanted me to have sex with this man because he is unable to pay his drug bill.

"Damien why can't I just pay what you owe? How much is it?

"Sugar Belle, it's five thousand dollars. I owe him a lot of money.

"Five-thousand dollars? I could not believe it.

A week later arrangements were made for me to sleep with Damien's drug dealer. I was to come to his high-rise apartment and spend an hour doing whatever he liked. I cannot believe that I agreed to do such a thing, but if it will stop all the drug use and get my man back, then I was going to do whatever I needed to do.

I entered the apartment on the fifteenth floor. It was very immaculate. There were white rugs on the floor, white leather furniture and a white dog walking around like he was the security. Damien's drug dealer was a short man with a large belly and probably a small dick. I didn't mean to think of him in those terms, but if it is small it won't matter. He asked me if I wanted a drink. I had an apple martini. He kept trying to make conversation, I wanted to get this over with. He asked about my life, I made up everything. I told him Damien and I met through a mutual friend and not the internet. He wasn't anyone that I should lie to anyway, but I did. After a few sips of my drink I started to feel light headed. My vision was blurred and about three other men had come out of a room, then I passed out.

When I woke up I was at home and Damien was standing

over me. I felt horrible. I felt like I had been drugged and I am not sure what happened. Damien told me that I had been sleep for three days. I was sore all over, I was unable to speak and I could not make any sense of anything. Damien came in my room with a glass of water and some medicine. I could not see what he was doing, but he said that this always makes him feel better. I was unable to move and Damien strapped my arm down on the bed. He then grabbed a needle and shot me up with it.

"Welcome to Euphoria", he said. I slowly started to fade.

DAMIEN

I really did not care too much for women. They were meant to be used. I had never had a long term relationship until I met Sugar Belle. She was innocent and sweet, but I wasn't. I was a drug dealer and a drug user. I had many drug ties and for many years, I was at the top of my game, but once I became a user, I fell into the user way of life.

I was born in San Francisco. I lived in Geneva Towers. The city was my life. I did not live in too many other places. My mom was a crack addict and my father was dead. I managed to graduate from high school and do three years of college. I also had a regular job for a minute, but it was not making me as much money as I was making on the streets. So I catered to the streets. I had cars, bitches, and drugs. Every day I lived the fast life, determined to never slow down. The life that I was living, was the life that was intended for me. I was determined to have it all and not look back. My drug habit started to take over my life. I ended up going to jail for about two years and I lost everything. Once I got out of jail I was on work furlough for three months. I needed to start working on some place to live.

I had been looking for a new chick to move in with. Managing women was a large job, but if her money was good then I was guaranteed. I had a few girls, but I needed a fresh new face, who was also innocent; that is how I found Sugar Belle. I had no intentions of falling in love with her; I just needed another place to stay and a warm body to lay next to. I started my search on MyBook; it was a place where everybody displayed all of their business to strangers without even asking. There were women desperately seeking a relationship. Instead of women complaining about men, you had more men complaining about women; the shit was banana's. It was very easy to find a woman who was looking, but not really looking. I made a few contacts, but some of these broads were too old. Some were even married and looking for something on the side. There were a lot of hoe's fishing and a lot of desperate men fishing too.

I contacted Sugar Belle. She responded and I did the usual. The sweet talking, dinner and hanging out. Spending time with her, giving her the attention she was lacking, while pretending that I had a job. After a few months, I moved in with her. I realized that she didn't have a lot of experience with worldly things. She never smoked or did drugs and she barely drank wine. I had to figure out another way to get her hooked. After a while I started to do more drugs than I had planned. It was hard to get Sugar Belle to do drugs. She would only look at me and pretended that I did not have this problem. She was very passive. It was strange because a passive person can either be at the end of exploding or on the verge. I needed her to stay balanced because I wasn't.

After a while I was no longer having sex with Sugar Belle, she annoyed me. She was just too good. She often prayed for me and I just continued to do my drugs. If she didn't give me money, I would literally tear the place apart to get what I needed. She loved me and I hated her for it. I had issues that she knew nothing about. I could not change at this moment; I was dealing with my life through drugs. I owed a lot of money to a lot of people and I wasn't sure how I was going to pay it. I needed a plan and I needed a plan quick.

I arranged to see my dealer, I owed him over five thousand dollars and I wasn't sure where the money would come from. I wanted to ask Sugar Belle, but I know that would be too much for her. I also needed to get high. My best bet would be to call Thelma. She was the local hooker. She always had dope, and if she didn't, she knew how and where to get it.

"What's up T, what cha' got?"

"Hey baby, what you need?"

"I need everything".

"Then you got it baby. Come pick me up in thirty minutes and we can go to your place and do what we do."

I guess my place would be cool since Sugar Belle would be at work. It was risky, but I didn't give a shit. I needed to get high and I needed to get high now. I drove to pick up Thelma and as usual she was in her typical over perfumed hoe gear. I had no intentions of actually fucking her, but she may be able to give me a blowjob or something. Nobody wants to admit fucking with a hoe, but people do it all the time, and then turn around and call a hoe a hoe, forgetting the fact that they just laid down with the hoe. Drugs have a tendency to create high-risk situations. You are performing at a level that would be considered crazy. You are given access to something that feels so good, but is so bad for you.

We were headed back to house when Thelma needed to stop and pick up cigarettes. With all the drugs that she had in the bag, who needs to smoke a cigarette. I stopped anyway. As I was pulling up to the store I saw Big Red. Big Red was the biggest dealer in our area. He always meant business and was rarely seen in public. I was hoping that he did not see me, but of course like all dealers, they see everyone and everything, especially if they owed money.

He motioned for me to come to his car. I was acting as if I did not know he was talking to me.

"Hey, get the fuck out the car and come over here!" That confirmed he was talking to me. I slowly got out the car because Big Red has a tendency to shoot people on the spot, especially over money. I have known people who have lost their lives over five dollars, so I was sure it would be nothing to get rid of my ass over five thousand.

"Hey man, what's up with my money? I gave you a pass because of our previous history, but damn, you haven't even made any attempt to pay me."

"Yeah umm see, I need some time man, I am not working and shit is crazy right now."

"Look like you living good man, you wit' that Sugar Belle. Let me have her for a night and I will forgive your debt."

"Aww man, I can't do that." As soon as I said that, Thelma hoe ass comes out the store and hops in the damn car. Big Red looks over at me and asked "You wit that, man? I know times are hard if you fucking with that bitch. Have Sugar Belle come my way. I could use a new one."

I jumped in the car and sped off. All I needed was to get high. This time Thelma had weed, meth and coke and we did it all. I was so loaded that Thelma was in the midst of giving me a blow job when we both fell asleep; but it was the cold water and the yelling and screaming from Sugar Belle that woke us up. I forgot where I was. I scrambled to get up and leave. I left with Thelma because she needed a ride back to her place. I slept at her place for a few weeks before I was able to get in good graces with Sugar Belle. I had time to think about how I was going to convince her to pay my debt. I know it was a serious thing to be considering and I had put her through so much shit it's going to take some serious buttering up to get her to do it. Besides, it was just a few minutes of sex. Shit, bitches fuck for less these days anyway.

I was finally able to come home. I did all the right things to make sure that she was comfortable with me again. I was no good for Sugar Belle, she was a real sweet woman and I was messing up her life by coming in like a vulture and taking all that is good from her. I wanted to be good, but I just did not have the power to kick this habit. The reality was I didn't want the power. I wanted drugs.

Me and Sugar Belle was going for a walk. It had been one of our better times and I was actually enjoying the moment until Big Red pulled up and demanded his money. The plan was for him or one of his boys to rough me up in front of Sugar Belle, but it seems his threat and intimidation was enough. She was pleading to pay, but once she found how much, she just cried.

When I told her that he wanted to have sex with her in order to pay my debt, she just cried even more. It took some convincing, but eventually she agreed.

I drove her there to be with my dealer. I was afraid for her, but I had snorted so many lines of coke, my reality had shifted and it was just another day at the office. I told her it would be ok and that I would return within an hour. I was almost ashamed for what was about to happen, but it needed to be done. I needed a fresh start and more money.

After an hour I went to pick up Sugar Belle. She had been drugged and was not awake enough to walk. Big Red looked at me and said, "Another long-term customer." They had drugged her drink and shot her up with heroin. A lot of heroin. I took her home and put her in the bed. I stayed with her and made sure she was still breathing. I wanted to have sex with her, but the smell of those men was still on her body. I looked at her while she slept, her life had changed, her face was different; no longer flushed and full of life.

When she woke up I was there. I looked at her with compassion because now she needed my help. I was finally able to relate to her, because now she was high and we shared this unacquainted love. In her eyes, I saw she needed me, so I grabbed her arm and told her she would be ok. I shot her up with some more heroin because there were customers waiting in the living room to sleep with her.

LIES

KEVEN

I am a man who enjoys fucking men. I have a relationship with a woman who I adore sometimes, other times I hate that I love her, hate that she is a woman and wish that I could change all this. There is something that a man gives me that she never will. There is an unfulfilled desire that is left lingering after I have been with a woman, that feeling never happens after I had been with a man. I am not sure if that makes me bi-sexual or just sexual. I have several children with whom I have lost contact with and she has no idea. The mothers of these children, some I remember, some I don't. Most of the time during sex I was either drugged up, super high or having some kind of out of body experience. You can say that I am fucked up. I had lived on the streets and in crack houses, since I was seven, it was almost like a second home. The instability became my normal. I have more family in jail than out. So what do you expect from a fatherless, motherless child who is now a man? Who is responsible for this shit? It's their fault, I didn't ask to come to this world. I have just been trying to make it all make sense.

I come from a broken home, never knew my dad and my mother just never got it together. She was either cracked out or sold out. I was forced to be the man and her man. I saw her turn from a loving kind mom, into a woman who hated me. I saw her change from a beautiful angel, who was my only hope, into a dismantled and broken woman. I no longer called her my mother, she was Martha to me. The woman she had become was a stranger. Her drug use had not only stolen her life but mine too. I lived in crack houses up until my uncle came and rescued me.

My uncle Ray ended up raising me until I was about 18. He was a gay man, and there was no shame in his game. I saw men coming in and out of his home. I heard them fucking at all times of the day and night, and he had no mercy. They would always come back for more. They were young and old, all kinds of races, no English, some English, married or single. He was the first male prostitute I had ever seen. I am not sure if that had an effect on me or not. He never tried to sway me or anything, but I would hear them having sex and it would turn me on. It would excite me. I guess that is where my adventure began. I wanted to know what it was like to be with a man; the unknown became my desire.

I guess at some point in my life I should have been more interested in girls, and I was, but they were not as easy as the boys. Finding a guy with your same sexual interest was like hitting the lottery. So I fucked a few girls here and there, but I loved the boys. My first was a dude from my neighborhood. He was the one that always had plenty of girlfriends, but he never stayed with them long enough to get attached. He would break hearts left and right. Every other weekend there would be some girl screamin' how she hated him, crying and begging to have him back. He would say, "Man you can't let these hoe's get next to you, a bitch will break you and then leave you". That obviously had been his story, but somewhere deep down I believed that just wasn't it. There was more to him than just not letting a bitch get close. I used that same excuse for not getting attached to women while loving men, and maybe that was his excuse too.

It all started one night when we were smoking weed and drinking. I had also started snorting coke, popping pills and anything else that would numb my existence. He was older than me and our conversation slowly went from girls to boys.

"Yeah man, I let this dope fiend suck my dick for some coke, it really ain't that bad ya' know"? No, I didn't know at the time, but I wanted to find out. He came over to me and grabbed my pants. I pretended to hesitate, but he knew I wanted him and so did I. As men, we always know when there is another one of us is in the room, we can smell it. I pretended to hesitate again, but this time, I gave in. I cannot tell you what it was like, but I can say we did everything imaginable that night, he was my teacher. I let him do whatever he wanted and I enjoyed all of it. It was a feeling I never experienced before. I mean, it's like I had fucked a girl once or twice, but it was not the same. I learned to fuck and conceal down to a science, no one would ever know, my homie was also my lover.

John had been my homie, lover, friend or whatever for many years. Square ass John is what they called him in the hood. We meet in our hood, did petty crimes together and often spent time in jail together. He was what I needed when I needed it. Most men would usually hook up with a woman and had relationships with men while in jail. We never did that; our relationship was what we did when we were out of jail. Neither of us really had a girlfriend, we were not really interested in any of that unless we needed a place to stay, money or some factor that was beneficial. The bitches in our neighborhood were just as trifling as the men. Everybody fucked with hoe's. And that's all women were, just hoe's or drug addicts. We never went on dates, never went too far out of our neighborhood, we just fucked with people in our hood, and robbed people out of it. Through it all, I wanted him in my life. I wanted him to be where ever I was. He was my best friend and what we did behind closed doors was our secret. I would remain loyal to him and him to me until the day we die. What we had was the closest thing to marriage, until I meet Elizabeth.

Elizabeth had a very nice smile. He eyes were piercing and inviting. I had no intention of starting anything with a woman, but there was something different about her. She was a nice curvy woman, although she seemed a little insecure about it, I loved that about her. A compliment here and there and she was on cloud nine. I was at the point in my life where I had realized that even in my least manly moments, I needed a woman to hold on to, so I watched her watching me.

At first, we had good times and great sex. I didn't have that much sexual experience when it comes to women, but according to all the books I read, they like to be put in the mood. Stuff like playing around and sucking on her nipples, or kissing her on the neck. Or rubbing on her clit, but not actually penetrating. Get her hot and wet, then provide her with some nice stiff dick. Every woman likes a hard dick. They like it to last a certain amount of time because it doesn't matter how big or long your dick is, if you are a minute man, that's all she is going to remember. You need to fuck a woman and put some shit on her mind.

I liked being with her. I was on her line, calling, texting her all the time, women like that shit. I knew I didn't deserve a woman like her, but I needed her to believe that she deserved a man like me. She accepted me and all my misfortune; somewhere deep I actually loved her. But, often my thoughts were with him. I knew that whenever I would get out of jail, John and I would be back at it. Whenever I had a chance to hang with my boy, we would get high, do some coke and have sex. As time went on something in me desired him more and her less, but I couldn't let go of either.

Elizabeth deserved better, she was a good woman, but she had chosen to love me. She cared for me and I loved her for it. Maybe one day I would marry her, that would be the right thing to do, but what kind of man was I for deceiving her this way? I was deceiving her even though I had told her on many occasions that I loved her. I was letting my moments of desiring a man dominate my existence, my future. And this drug habit was getting harder to hide. How long could this last? How can I let this go? How can I stop this when it had been with this man for so long? It was bound to cause a problem and I could not risk being exposed.

I had been home for a few weeks after doing 14 months on some fraud shit. She was doing her usual making breakfast then getting ready for work. I would get up and shower in the morning because John would always complain about her smell. She thought it was because I was getting ready to go out and look for a job. How could I be so careless? I knew as soon as she left, John would be coming over for our breakfast that she cooked. We would be fucking and sucking for most of the day, while she worked. That was the life I created, that was what I was doing and I did not want to know the alternative.

We were caught up in the moment. We were doing what we always do. Make small talk, snort some coke, smoke some weed and take Hennessey to the head. He would never ask about my relationship with her. He never complained because he was getting what he wanted. We even discussed increasing our cover by having him hook up with one of her friends. Since her best friend Tracy was forever single, maybe he could get with her. The problem was John did not like women at all. Not even to fuck them and Tracy did not like either of us.

It was a nice afternoon and John had arrived. We were watching the news for a bit before we were in the midst of doing what we do. I decided to move to the bedroom because Liz liked to have the shades open. There was a sound like someone entered the house. I became cautious, but we kept going. I was caught up in the moment and Liz would not be coming back for hours. Then it happened. There she was at the door, looking enraged, disappointed, shocked and confused. Every emotion created fire in her eyes, I knew immediately, the love had gone. She even looked like a different woman. I was so locked in on her eyes that I did not even notice the gun she was aiming at me.

Elizabeth

I love my man. He is the nicest guy I ever meet. He is very accommodating and always tries to make the best of everything. I just love him. There is nothing that I would not do for him. He makes love to me like no other man; my body is his canvas to do whatever he pleases.

Considering the other loser's that I have had in my life, he was my knight in shining armor. He was tall and somewhat skinny, with dark skin and green eyes. His hair was a black and shiny like licorice. He was a handsome, rugged man, life had not allowed him to be too pretty.

We met one day at the Berkeley Flea Market. I was just making a quick visit to pick up my favorite incense and jerk chicken. It was a hot day, so I was wearing my pink and white sun dress with no bra. Although I am on the heavier side, I wore my weight well. I haven't always been the most confident girl, but a good man that loves me and all my flaws changed all that. And there he was, standing by the group of men beating their drums to the sound of my heart. He stood out like a lit candle in a dark room. His smile meets my eyes and before I knew it we were talking about getting together and makin' things happen. His name was Keven.

I didn't rush to sleep with him. The first few weeks we did a lot of talking. My girlfriends hated him and were a bit surprised by this instant love affair. He was good to me and they were single and man less. My best girlfriend Tracy, went as far to think that he was a prime candidate for a down low brotha'. He dressed well and argued with her constantly. He had a best friend who always was anti-social. Just seemed to always be hangin' around for no reason except to just be with his "boy". That shit meant nothing to me, I had no reason to be concerned. She was my friend, had been since the 3rd. grade. She had been there through break-ups and make-ups and get back together's. There was no fighting me without fighting her too. So when it came to her opinion, I gave her the benefit of the doubt and listened to her rant. "Are you serious about this guy? I mean really serious? Tracy would ask those questions in disbelief at least once a month. I would confess that "Yes! For the umpteenth time, I love him, he is fine, he is mine and I am happy with him. So why can't you just be happy for me"? We both understood what happens when one friend gets a man and the other remains single. I just wish she didn't have to voice her opinion so much. I know that Keven had been in and out of jail since he was a teenager, he didn't have a job, not much education, but he did what he could. So when he got caught up in this identity theft sting, it was not a problem for me to wait the 18 months of time he had to serve in Santa Rita. Tracy would say, "I don't know Liz, this guy just seems a bit off. Two years no job? What does he do, just fuck you good? I just smiled, only I needed to know the answer to that.

Of course, he was a great lover. When we first met, he

lived between my legs. I can't remember a time when I was so sexually satisfied. Keven would barely eat my pussy, but he would play in it like it was his soft, wet playground. He would stick his finger in my pussy then slowly insert his other finger in my ass, while he licked my clit. Complete sexual satisfaction. I would cum all over the place, so by the time he entered me I was wetter than a puddle. Sex with him was simple yet explosive. He would enter me slow and deep. Only stopping when he reached the end. Then he would hold it there and pull back only a bit to penetrate my spot then entered me again. I loved it. Maybe I was in love with the sex because it was damn good. Making love to him was like having our souls combust, then release. All I needed was a moment with him, the thought of him being inside me lasted forever.

This would be the longest time that we were ever apart. I felt like I was doing time too. The weekend visits and the talk of marriage kept me interested and satisfied. My sexual needs were meet with some good batteries and a bullet. He looked good, kept himself up and always made me feel like I had something to look forward to. He wrote the most romantic letters, he said the most wonderful things, and I was falling more and more in love with this man.

During his time away, I got in shape and lost thirty-five pounds. I got promoted to Manager at my job and moved into a larger apartment with hopes of having children one day. I saved my money because I knew that when my baby came home he would need the money to make a fresh start. Usually, when he came home he would always live with his best friend John, but this time he was coming home to me. I will get him a new outfit so when he came home we would go out and celebrate. It had been over a year and he would be home early for good behavior.

A few weeks before Keven was released I started receiving text messages on my phone to "**Leave Him Alone**". When I called the phone number there was just an anonymous voice message. There were notes left on my car saying, "He's mine, he'll never be completely yours". At first, I thought this was some sick joke from one of my friends. We had all been kickin' it tough since his lockup and they knew I would be unavailable when he came home, so I thought nothing of it. But when I came home from work and there was a note saying that I was a "**Dead Bitch**", I immediately took notice. It was no longer a joke or funny and I was pissed. I had always kept a gun in my home. I was stalked by an x-boyfriend who I eventually had to put in jail. He was abusive and I came home too many times with him sitting in my living room with a pistol in his hand. Now I lived alone and I needed it for protection, I would never be a victim again, so I kept it loaded.

During my next visit with Keven, I told him what was happening. He said he had no idea who this could be. How could he? He was in jail and I wasn't going to let it spoil my moment with him. I was preparing a lot of things for us. I was looking forward to us spending the rest of our lives together, so whoever the hell this was, was going to have to deal with that. Although I appeared to be secure in our relationship, I did wonder who this nuisance could be. Keven had been in jail for over a year, had he started a relationship with someone and made her the same promises he made me? It sure would be possible, because sometimes that is what men do. Especially the ones that go to jail frequently. These questions started to clog my brain, but I wasn't going to let it spoil his homecoming.

The day had arrived. Keven was coming home and I was more than elated. I had taken some days off work just to be with him. I took a long hot bath, put on some clean sheets and prepared to pick him up. As I walked to my car I noticed another note, this time it just said **"Stupid"**. I just didn't get it, but I was not worried. Maybe it was an old girlfriend that had resurfaced or a mad woman whom he had had a previous relationship with, I don't know. He had no children, so there was absolutely no baby mama drama. Whoever it was, it was too bad for them because I was going to pick him up and tonight he would be in my bed.

As I waited for him to come out, I thought about the time we meet, all the love we made and how good he was to me. He was my best friend and I could not wait to show him how devoted I had been. Before I knew it, he was standing there knocking on the window of the car, I unlocked the door. It was hard to contain myself. He looked the same, maybe gained a little weight. He smiled and gave me a kiss. He appeared to be happy to see me but looked as if something else was on his mind. He was here, but not really here with me.

"What's wrong baby"

"Nuthin', just hungry" Being on the outside again always takes an adjustment, happy to see you though baby".

"Oh good", I fried some chicken with greens and cornbread".

"Ok, yeah, Ya' mind if John comes by, you know he's my dog and I haven't seen him in a minute".

"Oh sure, no problem". I was thinking, what the fuck? You haven't seen me in a minute neither and I have vagina jewels, what the hell was this?

The drive home was silent. That was the beginning and the end of our conversation. Why the hell did he have to see John today? What was the urgency? Now that he was coming over, I all of a sudden was not in the mood, not excited and the thrill just died. All this was for him and he wanted his friend to come over? I wanted him to be happy and besides we would have all night to make it up, so I guess I didn't mind that much, but why?

John came by and we ate and watched old episodes of Martin, it was a marathon weekend. Keven and John just talked about people in the hood. They talked about the who, what, when and where almost all night. I was completely bored and felt left out, I could not wait until he left. When I felt myself getting sleepy, I realized that it was almost one in the morning and John was still here. I was completely annoyed. When Keven finally came to bed, he mentioned John was too drunk and needed to sleep it off on the couch. I was even more annoyed, but the fact that Keven went straight to sleep left me even more heated. I needed to get laid and why didn't he? I was pissed off, but I guess he needed to rest and there was this adjustment factor to consider.

A few days went by and I was returning to work. John had been visiting every day. I hope this comes to an end soon because he is the last person I want to see when I come home. Keven and I were finally able to make love, and it was ok, not as passionate as I thought it would be. For a man who had been locked up for over a year, I thought we would be going round after round at least 3 or 4 times. We only had sex once.

I got dressed for work and cooked him breakfast like I always do before I leave. I know things would get better, he is just getting used to being on the outside. Tonight, when I get home I will cook him a nice dinner and make him remember what it is to be with me. Being locked up with a lot of knuckleheads day in and out will sometimes make you lose touch with the real world. I would go home for lunch for a quickie and give him the real deal later when I get off work.

I quickly left work anticipating what was to come. He did not have the biggest penis, but he definitely worked what he had, and I loved it. I was missing that part of him. As I walked into my home, I smelled cologne. I thought my baby must have been in the shower. That's even better. I would attack him, while he was butt naked. As I got closer to my bedroom I noticed unfamiliar clothes on the floor, and what sounded like a struggle or something; nothing too loud, but very noticeable. Was my baby in trouble? I kept my gun in the hallway closet, so I slowly grabbed it. I tiptoed back down the hallway and slowly opened my bedroom door and God could not have prepared me for what I saw. It was Keven fucking John. It was all in slow motion, seeing my man having the look of complete pleasure on his face, while he fucked a man he called his best friend. Everything went black, I heard four shots and when the smoke cleared there were two dead bodies on the bed.

When the smoke cleared, there was my man and John dead

on the bed. I stood there in complete shock. My body went numb. My life had flashed before me and I was no longer the woman I was. I do not know how much time passed before I decided to call the police. I had to think, I had to swallow what I had just done. I was deceived. I was angry and sad. I had no words that could express what I was feeling. I could not wake him and ask why he did this to me. I could not ask him all the questions that were being asked in my head. Whatever I gave or hoped for was all gone in an instant.

I wanted to cry but no tears would come. I dropped the gun and just sat there on my knees, surrounded by black space. My mind reverted to the first time we meet, kissed or even touched. I realized how magical a deception can be. I no longer knew where anything was in my home, I was paralyzed. I could hear the sirens, they were coming for me and there was nothing I could do about it. I would tell them the truth. I would tell them it was not what it looked like. Even with those thoughts, I had yet to have a voice. I could not speak and I was being devoured by my thoughts and of the images that were before me. Disbelief, how did I miss such a thing? How did I welcome this in my life? My imperfections amplified in an image that was not recognizable. How after all these years, had I been so blind? I had allowed him to determine my fate, and now I had determined his.

As I heard the police enter my home, I just could not bear what was to come. How could I live? The embarrassment, the betrayal, the loss and going to jail for a double murder. All of this for love. Love has caused my blindness, I closed my eyes to reality and woke up to this fantasy. All I wanted was to be loved and taken care of. I don't deserve this; I can't believe what I have done. The trial, the media, the jail time; voices were now in my head and in my home; the gun went off one more time.

SASHA

I have been with Frank for seven years. I loved him, but I wasn't sure if he loved me. After two kids and no ring, I wasn't sure if I still wanted to be married to him. Frank was not the easiest person to get along with. All he did was take, blame and accuse. He traveled a lot for work and maybe that's where all the time went. I spent most of it waiting. Waiting for him to come home, waiting for him to marry me, waiting for him to finally love me the way I deserved. Seven years and I never felt so empty. This must come to an end.

We meet in 2009 in Atlanta. It was during a time of transition's, beginnings and endings. I was really trying to find myself. I was trying to figure how to find my place in the world. I had moved from California and been in Atlanta for six months and nothing was happening for me. I could not get a job. My money was running out and I was partying way too much. I was also doing a lot of shopping. On this particular day, I had left a job interview and decided to treat myself with something from the mall. There he was, walking through Lennox mall with a lot of bags. I didn't mean to stare, but I did. I was wondering why he had all those bags. Who were they for? And how can I get a few?

We caught eyes. "You want to help with these bags? he said.

"Is there anything in there for me"? "Yes", he said. "Everything is yours". And just like that, we were together. Jacob was not what I normally would be attracted to, but his confidence was attractive. That moment changed the whole course of my life and my intention of finding myself. My ship went off course and it would spend the next seven years in a complete storm. I found myself in love with a man that could charm the panties off any woman. He would fill your head with compliments then play with your insecurities. He'll send you a few gifts to make you feel special, so when the love starts to burn you wouldn't remember. Once you are caught up in his web, the pain of staying and the pain of leaving becomes one in the same, so you stay. You stay because of the kids, the financial security and the unknown.

I wanted to become a legal secretary but had dropped out of school when I got pregnant with our first child Jaylen. The plan was for me to be home with Jaylen for six months, then go back to school. Once I was home with our baby, Jacob started to go out a lot. He would come home at one and two in the morning, or not be seen for weeks because of work. I stayed home with a new baby and I was clueless. When we talked about me going back to school, we always ended up arguing.

"Why do you want to go back to school? You have a baby now, you are a mother and should stay at home with the baby. You have everything you need right here."

"I have a baby? We have a baby. But it seems since our baby got here, you have forgotten that!

"Forgot? How can I forget when all you do is text me all day asking where I am at and when I am coming home? You need to find something else to do besides bother me all day. And lower your voice when you talking to me."

"Lower my voice?" Are you fuckin' serious? You ain't my daddy and I am leaving."

Before I knew it Jacob had jumped up and he was so close to my face that I could smell the Jack Daniels on his breath. It was his favorite drink. He held my neck so tight I thought I would pass out. The look in his eyes was from someone I did not recognize. He was so furious that the only thing that made him remove his hand from my neck was Jaylen. He started to cry. He was only 8 months old at the time, but that day he saved my life.

As I sat on the floor Jacob looked down on me in a matter of fact kind of way and said, "Look, Sasha don't ever think about leaving me. I will kill you first." Then he left.

That was the first time Jacob put his hands on me and I feared he would do it again. The verbal insults were everyday life, but this time he snapped. I had never seen him so angry. It made me believe that something else was going on with him. The control, the possessiveness, the monitoring where ever I went became more than I can handle. Since I said I was leaving him, he has been more than possessive. He took my keys to the car, my ATM card, and I could only use my cell phone when he was around. I was trapped. I became a zombie inside. This went on for three long years, then I found out I was pregnant again. I was happy to be blessed with another child. Jaylen had been an amazing little boy. A little sister or brother would make great company, but my living situation had to change.

During my pregnancy, Jacob let up a little on my restrictions. I was able to freely go to my doctor's appointments with my cell phone. He was always working late, still coming home at all times of the night. I was carrying our baby alone. He would check on me from time to time, but Jacob and I were drifting more and more apart. I no longer loved him. I wanted to get away from him and it was time to start planning. I knew he would not allow me to have too much time on my phone, so I had to capitalize on every opportunity.

I called my sister in Texas. I had to let someone know what was going on. I was living in hell covered with sugar and I needed a way out. My plan was to leave him and move to Texas with my sister. This is not the life I want for myself. My children deserved better and so did I. This would take meticulous planning because Frank is very noisy. He likes to double check shit and watch the house for hours. He was stalking me, even when I was at home with nowhere to go. Why had he changed so much? There was so much love in the beginning. I fell so deep in love with him that I knew it would last forever. I don't understand making all that effort to get a woman, just to treat her like shit. What's the point? He never wanted to marry me, he has me locked up in the house most of the time, the verbal and emotional abuse, I can't take it anymore. When will it end? It won't end. I have to end it. I have to stand up for myself and my children.

I was six months pregnant. I had a few more weeks before I was making my move to Texas. I had to make sure everything was normal. My day to day routine had to remain the same. Next month my doctor's appointments will be scheduled every two weeks. I let my doctor know that I was moving to another state and if he could make a referral. He never met Jacob, so he thought I was a single mother moving closer to family for support. I needed everything to be in place, so when I got on that plane, I would not have a reason to look back.

I begin to send small boxes of our things to my sister. Every time I had an appointment or needed something, I also made a stop to the post office. I had my sister purchase the plane tickets and send them to my email. I opened another bank account in my name and slowly started to move money from our account to mine. I only paid the mortgage and the other bill money was going directly into my account. By the time he figured out anything, I would be long gone. I planned on having at least ten-thousand dollars in the bank before I left. That's all I would need to start over. I wanted to go back to school and live a normal life. I had to free myself from his prison.

I tried to continue with everyday life as much as possible. I didn't want to be too nice or too distant. I wanted him to believe that I still loved him and that I would never leave him. There were times that I could have killed Jacob in his sleep. I would just look at him and not know the man that he was now. A figment of the old Jake. I would think about my life and how things had changed between us. What happened? I had no real clue. There was a time when he was the love of my life. He made me so happy. We were inseparable, and then he changed. He seemed to be irritated all the time. I could never do anything right. He would complain about everything. Was it the kids? Was it because I wanted to be married? He made enough money for the both of us. He has always been a great provider. He loved his son and that's one of the reasons why the decision to leave has been so hard. My son loves his father, but his father does not love me. The turmoil I am feeling is draining. And being pregnant does not help. I have to make a decision that will be the best for me. I am not sure if I want to see Frank again, but how do I tell that to our son? Do I want my son to grow up in a house where his father abuses his mother? He is young now, but I cannot imagine the long-term effects of him seeing his father yell and belittle his mother on a daily basis. I wanted him to see us happy, but the possibility of that happening was slim. I have to leave to save his and my life.

I was sitting in the closet surrounded by clothes when the reality of what was happening to us made me reflect on my life. I wanted Jacob to be a great father and my husband. He wanted to be neither. I never knew who my father was. I grew up in an abusive home. I saw my mother bloodied and bruised up on several occasions and here I am facing the same situation. I wish that I could call my mother and tell her that I loved her and needed her right now. But the abuse left her unloved and unable to love. She only thought about herself and nothing else mattered. It has been five years since I have seen or talked to her. All I knew was that she was on her fourth marriage. Jaylen has never met his grandmother, but she could care less. My child was facing the same shame that was placed on me. The shame of another mother's son, and my son does not know his grandmother because of it.

As a young girl, it was boyfriend after boyfriend. I was looking for love, I can't tell you how many times I was raped of that chance. Every time I thought I found love, it would slip away. I would get high and come down, still looking for another hit. My love drug habit started in high school. I was dumped by my high school sweetheart for a girl that gave blowjobs. I learned how to give blowjobs. I just knew that would help me keep a man and it did for maybe an extra few weeks. I was sucking more dick than Jenna Jamison. I just knew that was what all men wanted. Soon after, I was cheated on by a boy who told me he loved me. HE fucked me good, left stacks on the dresser. He looked me in my eyes and gave me whatever I wanted, then went out and did the same thing with two other girls. I remember dating a guy that played for the Oakland Raiders. He was built like a god. I nicknamed him Adonis. I had access to all the finer things in life, but after nine months, I wasn't being sexual satisfied. Fucking him was like having a mouse nibble at my pussy, continuously. His penis was a midget and I could not deal with that. I was annoyed and alone most of the time and it left me even more hungry for the ultimate love.

Dating was never easy. And as you get older shit gets more strange and weird. I dated an old man once, and again it all boiled down to the sex. He was fun to be with, talk to, but sexually the lovemaking was heavy and he talked to himself a lot. "Take this good dick" Take it this good dick." I had to literally close my eyes and shake my head. Like, how did I get so lucky? I eventually ended the relationship, it just wasn't enough chemistry or dick to keep me interested. I had him pay a few bills and then ended the relationship. Then there was Michael. Michael was amazing. Whenever I saw him all we did was ravish each other. He was an artist, so he lived life as a free spirit. Spreading love to whoever would spread their legs. I was in love with him. I thought me accepting his desire to spread love, would eventually show him that I loved him and that I was loyal. He would always come back to me. Yes, he would always come back to me, because I was always available for him to come back. Never once did being a fool cross my mind. It wasn't that he loved me or even thought I was special. I was convenient. I made it easy for him to fuck up and return whenever he wanted.

One night Michael was complaining that we never spend time together. He was mostly a night owl and I worked during the day. I decided to surprise him one day for lunch, so I showed up at his house with food. I rang the doorbell and he didn't answer. He usually would sleep all afternoon, so I went through the backyard and through the back door. I noticed that there were two empty wine glasses, maybe he had friends over last night. As I walked up the stairway leading to his room, I heard noises. I could not tell what it was, it seemed as if he was talking to someone, but very faint. I opened the door and there he was fucking another woman. I immediately closed the door and ran down the stairs. Michael ran after me yelling, 'What are you doing here?" "What am I doing here? I was screaming, what the fuck are you doing? It isn't enough that you cheat on me, but you have to bring the bitch to your home and fuck her in the same bed we fuck in?" I was beyond livid, but it was the pain I needed to finally move on.

I was trying to use the shelf to get off the floor when I noticed a long black box. It was stuffed in the back of the closet, behind Jacob's clothes. It was something that I never noticed before and obviously paid no attention to. The lid was sealed shut, but after a few minutes of prying, it opened. There were pictures inside of a family with kids. At first, I did not recognize Jacob in the pictures. I had never met any of Frank's family members, so initially, I assumed that these pictures were of his sister and her children. As I continued to go through the pictures I noticed that Frank was looking a bit more intimate with the lady that I thought was his sister. The children looked almost like Jaylen. I noticed that they both had on wedding rings. I turned over one of the pictures and it read, "*Mr. and Mrs. Goldberg 5th Wedding Anniversary.*" Was Jacob married with another family? Is this why he couldn't marry me? What the hell is going on here? I was upset and crying. I was sitting on the floor holding my belly, trying to comprehend what was going on. I reached for my phone to call him, but first, I needed to calm down. I could not believe that I had spent seven years with someone who was already married. Why did he do this to me? A wife and kids? He has been playing us both for seven years. I had reached my breaking point, I would not be lied to, cheated on or fucked over again. I had to end this. My life has been a river of constant disappointment's in life and in love, I could not take it anymore.

JACOB

Sasha was the most beautiful black woman I had ever met. Her dark skin was smooth and her hair was long and black. She was walking towards me in what seemed like slow motion. She was slim, with nice boobs. I had no idea what I would say when she passed by. I just knew that I needed to say something and not sound corny in the process. Just looking at her made we want her, so when our eyes locked; it made me forget that I was shopping for my wife.

Up until that point, I had never dated a black woman. I had always been curious about them, had a few black friends, but never a black woman. My Jewish upbringing never mentioned anything about dating outside my race. It was assumed that after college I would end up with a nice Jewish girl and live life as such. And that is exactly what happened, but that was not what I wanted. I was attracted to black women. I remember in the third grade there was this girl named Myesha. I would always share my lunch with her. Even when she refused, I always had it ready for her. She was so smart and beautiful, just different than anything I ever saw. That was my first crush, after elementary I didn't see her anymore, but being with someone like her had always been on my mind.

You go through life with one thing in mind, only to end up

with another. I married that nice little Jewish girl, had a few kids, but life was hell. I did not love my wife and she just loved my wallet. I met Ashley in college. She was your typical white suburban brainwashed girl. She grew up with a silver spoon in her mouth and thought the world revolved around her. She often spoke about the atrocities of the world. She volunteered in Africa and for several non-profit organization that catered to the needs of the less fortunate. Then she would come home and complain about the young black man in the elevator or the parking lot. She was a real poster child for the white and privileged. She wore me down for this marriage. I wanted someone else. I married her and had affairs, but once I met Sasha, I fell in love. I wanted to tell her that I was married, but I thought that would be the end of our relationship, so I lied to keep her and I lied to control her. I was already married, a divorce at this point would be too messy. My wife would take me for all I got, especially after she finds out that I have another son. After a year of dating, Sasha got pregnant with Jaylen, so I bought her a house in Stone Mountain. I lived in Savannah with my wife, which was more than three hours away. I had to keep my schedule in order. I am a businessman; I owned and sold many businesses's and my schedule was very hectic. I traveled a lot on the east and west coast and had have been able to maintain two households for over seven years. The stress of it all is wearing on me, but I do not want to give up either one. I have started drinking and partying trying to ignore the chaos of my life, but when I go to either home, it is a constant reminder that I created this.

I love Sasha but I cannot give her what she wants. She wants to be my wife. All I can do is provide for her financially and hope that she never leaves me. I could not let her leave me because she is the one that I love. My wife could leave me and I would not shed a tear, but the cost would probably leave me poor. Although she was very educated, she never worked a day in her life. After ten years of marriage, and two daughters, she would get me for everything she could.

My wife is a true Housewives fan. She watched the show like it was her life. It was like she wanted to up the girls on TV, by spending money, getting plastic surgery and Botox. She was a nice looking blond, but the surgeries were causing the opposite effect. She was aging and not as beautiful. I still had sex with her because that was the only thing we really connected on. She was a freak in bed. She liked anal and loved it when I fucked her in the mouth. There was nothing like watching your dick go in and out of a mouth, it didn't matter who's mouth it was. I enjoyed those moments, but it was not enough to keep me faithful. After sex, we both rolled over in opposite directions. There was no intimacy afterward or conversation.

I was driving to Stone Mountain, trying to get home to see Jaylen. He was growing up right before my eyes. As soon as I walked in, Sasha and I had an argument. We hardly ever argued over anything, but this particular day, I had been on the road for over five hours and I just wanted to relax. She started to complain about me never being home and raising our son alone. Coming home at different times of the night basically left her a single mother. I was too tired to try to explain my schedule or to justify my lying. She was yelling and the baby was sleep. I don't know what happened, something snapped in me when I heard her say that she was leaving me. I jumped up and grabbed her neck and threaten to kill her. I had invested too much of my time and money in order for her to leave me now. It had been seven years and she wasn't going anywhere. I took everything that would allow her to leave me, credit cards, keys and any cash that was in the house. I had to control her every move in order for her not to think it was a good idea to try and leave me.

In all of the seven years we had been together, she never said she was going to leave me. Where was this coming from? The next morning, she told me she was pregnant again. I could not believe it; Jaylen had just turned six years old. I could not let her leave me. What more did she want? There wasn't much conversation between us. She looked at me with those beautiful eyes, but I no longer saw love, there was a sadness that I knew that I had caused.

I wasn't sure what I was going to do anymore. If Sasha was thinking of really leaving me, she could. I know that I could not really stop her, but I did not want that. I wanted her to stay with me. I could not live without her and there was nothing that I would do in order to keep her in my life. I was wrong and maybe I should come clean and tell her that I am married. I would get a divorce and live my life with her.

"I am sorry", I said. But she did not respond. She just looked at me in disbelief. I kissed her on the forehead and left for work. I had to be in New York for three days.

SASHA & JACOB

I was two months away from my due date. When I first found out that I was having another son, I was elated. I wanted another son, I wanted Jaylen to be a big brother. I looked at the sonogram and I was in tears. Tears of happiness that Jaylen was having a baby brother, tears of sadness because he probably would not grow up having his father near. I wanted to have a family that included both parents. I wanted my children to know their father. I wanted to be with him because deep down inside, I longed for him, the love that we had. I wanted him to be the Jacob that I had met at the mall. I wanted him to love me like I loved him, but his absence did not allow our love to be anything more than what it was.

I had moved most of my personal things out of the house. Jacob had not taken any notice because he was hardly there. I was moving on and I could not look back. If Jacob wanted anything with me, he would have to come to Texas and get it. I was tired of trying to be something to someone that didn't even love me enough to make me his wife. I was having his second child and I all I wanted was for us to be a family. Love had eluded me again. I decided that I would just raise my children and put being a relationship on the back burner. I had had it with love. I had already spent seven years with a man who said he loved me, but couldn't show me in the way I needed him too. I wanted a new life and a new beginning. I could not wait to get to Texas to breathe in some fresh air.

I found a three-bedroom home in Houston. My sister helped me find a home near where she lived. I loved my sister. She was the only one that wasn't jealous of me. I had a brother who I lost contact with years ago. My mom had several kids all over and none of our dads were ever a part of any of our lives. Whether she was married to them or not, they all eventually left. I would not have to raise my children alone. I had family in Texas. Family that I had been alienated from since I met Jacob and I could not wait to see them. I will miss my home in Stone Mountain. I never was a social person, but I enjoyed the simple life that the south had to offer. I knew that I had to make this change. I deserved a better life. I deserved to be loved. I still had my desire to be loved, still searching to find something in someone that I probably should find in myself. I am not sure if I know what love means anymore. For now, I'll just be the best mom I can.

Sasha's reaction to my kiss left me feeling like she needed me to be there with her. I was to be in New York for the next three days, but I may just cut my trip short just to be with her and Jaylen. She was expecting another baby and I really haven't been spending as much time as I could with the both of them. I stay away because of the guilt that I feel. Every day I am pretending that we have this great relationship and I am a great father when I have been cheating on my wife and deceiving Sasha. I probably should make her my wife and get a divorce and hopefully, everything will be fine.

I called Sasha to check on her and Jaylen, but there was no answer. I didn't leave a message so I can surprise them. I arrived on Wednesday night and Sasha still had not answered the phone. I took Uber from the airport. When I arrived at the house, there was a moving van in front of the house. Sasha did not mention that she was moving anywhere, so I was confused as to why a moving van would be front of the house. When I walked in Sasha was at the dinner table, crying and upset with some pictures spread all across the table. As I got closer I noticed that the pictures were of me and Ashley. It must have been during happier times before I met Sasha. I immediately went into panic mode. There was no denying the fact that I was married and I had been lying to Sasha for the last seven years.

"Baby, I am sorry."

"Why are you sorry Jacob?"

"I didn't want you to find out this way."

"It's been seven years Jacob. I don't think you wanted me to find out at all".

I stared at the man I wanted to be my husband and I could not see his face. I was looking at a man with no soul who had betrayed me and his son. The rage in me was so deep, that all I could do was talk in a whisper. I did not have a voice to yell or show my anger. I was seven months pregnant, being with this man has not been easy and all he can say is that he didn't want me to find out this way!

I stood up to walk away, I wanted to check on my son, but Jacob insisted on talking. I did not want to talk. He followed me and I was pleading with him to leave.

"Jacob, I am leaving you. It's over between us. I do not want anything from you."

"Sasha no, you can't do this!" I am sorry." I was getting a divorce. I was going to tell her about you and our kids."

"Well, you are seven years too late. I am leaving and I am taking my son, and don't bother trying to find us."

I turned to walk away and Jacob grabbed me by the arm. I feared for my life, I thought he would try and choke me again. I was trembling, I was not strong enough to fight him off. He was pulling me towards him and as I about to face him, I stabbed him in the chest. The look in his eyes was disbelief, then his eyes became glassy and he was holding his chest while falling to his knees. He looked up and was reaching his hand out to me, "I love you, why did you stab me?" I looked him in the eyes and said, "It been seven years of neglect, deception, lies and you say you love me. Well, I wouldn't stab you if I didn't love you".

I left Jacob bleeding on the floor. I wrapped the knife in a kitchen towel and packed it with my belongings. There was nothing that was going to stop me from making this move.

LUST

STEPHAN GREEN

My name is Stephan Green. I am the CEO of Telkom Communications. I started this company from the ground up and I am very proud of its accomplishments. I am a Harvard graduate. Although the name, Harvard carries prestige, I am more proud of what I've done after college. I have a wife; her name is Sarah. Sarah is the perfect housewife, mother, and friend, I used to love her, but now I just care. I have given her the life that she deserves; I have provided a smooth and comfortable transition from her humble beginnings to a life of luxury. On the outside, we look like the typical suburban couple. She is the President of the PTA, very busy with the children and I have created another life that better suits my desires.

All my life I have worked. I have done what my father did for my mother. That is all that was asked of me right? My parents could only give me what they received and I had it down to a science. I would mimic what they did, it was my best example and appeared to work for them. My mother appeared to be a happy woman, but my father had numerous affairs, numerous children, yet my mother remained, she stood by his side and loved him until he died. I wanted my wife to be present, but then again, I did not. I wanted her to act like she loved me like she did when we first meet, but instead she spent my money to show her appreciation. I had no real connection to my children, they took on the attitude of their mother. I was the human ATM. Family vacations were far and few in between. A couple of years after the twins' birth things just began to spiral down. I knew I was pretending on the inside, I knew that my desire to have Shelly would eventually tear us apart, but I was willing to take that chance. Take the chance on a life that I could never have in public. A life that would become the reason I lived. I loved my children and I even at times loved my wife, but that only fulfilled a very small part of my existence. Shelly made me feel complete.

Shelly is a tall beautiful woman. She is my desire. She makes me feel like I could conquer the world. It was something that my wife lacked. I am not sure if she believed that I could accomplish what I have or that she was even happy that I did. I did what was expected, but for me, that left an empty space. She was warm and attentive. She asked questions and showed sincere interest. Then we would make love at the same place at the same time and the same hotel day in and out, weekends or whenever I could get a moment with her. She was my drug and I was addicted. There will be no rehab for me. Who cares that each time I saw her she requested two-thousand dollars for her company. I could afford it and I would take her until my soul died. For me, there was nothing else. Before her my life was dying, suicide was a thought. Without her, I would die. She was the fuel I needed to tolerate my existing life. When I talked of a future, she would always tell me to stay with my wife, so I did.

"Hi, Darlin', how are you today?" Shelly would ask. She always wanted to know how "I" was doing and I liked that. If Sarah were to ask me how I was doing, it would be a precursor to asking for more money, or a new car or something that she needed to make herself look better.

"How about dinner at The Garden?" I asked Shelly during one of our phone calls that never lasted more than two minutes.

"I would love to", she said. "See you at seven." She knew my habits. She knew that if I wanted to take her to dinner and it was a Wednesday, 7 would be the perfect time for us. Tonight, I would have two hours to spare. Sarah would be working out with her trainer; the kids would be with their nanny, so I had the time.

The Garden was a small Italian restaurant located on the outside of south San Francisco. It was nestled between the bay and Glendale Park.

It was very personal, very private and romantic. Each booth has a view of the San Francisco bay. That was our place. After dinner, we would find ourselves deeply involved with an affair that was more than just sex. An affair that begins each time we saw each other. We conversed about worldly things that spread across globes; politics, music, love, life, and public policies. I rarely talked about my personal life. She punished me with her intelligence. I loved her and I think she loved me, though she never said it. She never had to, this felt like the perfect love. It did not matter if she did or didn't. I never had to hear her tell me she loved me. The last time I heard I love you from my wife, it had no meaning, empty words that held no weight in my heart.

Shelly did things to me that made my soul stir. Her touch felt like a magic wand. Where ever her hand touched, I was healed. She would tie me up and blindfold me. The unknown became my weakness and it made me high. She pulled all my strings, and I let her torture me until I ejaculated. When our bodies were in motion it was natural and in sync, going where only a breeze could find. When we were apart, I thought of her like an unopened box of pleasures. A box that only opened for me, filled with undeserved pleasures. Soon this will be over and my perception would become my reality. My vision would clear and I would be back living the American dream with my wife.

I arrived home a little after 10 p.m. The kids were in bed and my wife was at the computer as usual. I never knew what she did during this hour and I never asked. We would sit and have simple conversations about our day, the kids and plans for the week. As she talked I would look at her knowing where I had been, knowing that soon this illusion of a life would be over. For a moment I thought of where had the free-spirited woman I'd married gone? I remember something happening, but not sure exactly what. She became distant and I gave her space. I longed for something that she could no longer give me and now that I am getting it from someone else, her voice just sounded like empty space, sound with no meaning. I guess I looked interested, somewhere deep inside I really wanted to be present, but I just wasn't and one day I would not be able to pretend. We gave each other a peck goodnight and I got into the shower looking forward to my next moment with Shelly.

Worked was filled with last minute meetings, and because

my company did not reach its forecasted profits, there were talks of a merger with a rival company. I wanted to wait it out before making any irrational decisions. I had my assistant book me a week's vacation in the U.S Virgin Islands, I needed time to think. Maybe I could also send my wife away with her friends, while I unwind with Shelly.

Shelly insisted we had separate rooms, which I agreed. It would be nothing for my wife to check up on me. Even though I did not take that many business trips, she would always check on me, making sure that I was where I said I was. Yet, she never asked to go or asked why she wasn't invited. I told her this time that I was going to a business venture retreat with management. She opted to go to Napa with her friends. Although I never meet any of her friends, I assumed they were much like her. I did know she spent a lot of money on these trips with her friends. All that did not matter, she was out of the way and I was on my way to my self-made paradise.

The time spent with her was lovely. We laughed and partook in several brands of expensive liquor. Shelly could consume a lot of alcohol, but never showed it. If I didn't know better, I would have thought her to be an alcoholic. I've never seen her drink so much. I wondered if something was wrong. I took her shopping, had more dinner and drinks and we were in for the night. It was the third day, and when she woke up and looked at me, and decided it was time she went home. I didn't question her decision although I wasn't ready for her to go. I guess all of our fun had been had. I decided to stay a few more days and head home early Friday.

When I arrived home, it was late in the evening. I stopped by my office to check on things and headed home. When I arrived, there was no one home, so I assumed Sarah and the kids were still gone. The emptiness of the house was an example of what I felt when I was in it. I took a long hot shower and decided to watch a movie. I do not remember the last time that I sat in my home and watched a movie. I can't remember a time that I actually wanted to be at home. I put on my robe and went down to the den to look for something to watch. There were tons of movies, I did not know we had such a collection. There were several movies for the kids, the time I must have missed. There were old movie classics like Beverly Hills Cop with Eddie Murphy and Taxi with Robert DeNiro and Reservoir Dogs. I would just watch as many as I could, maybe something like Reservoir Dogs or Unusual Suspects. I also noticed a black box with several unlabeled movies in it, so I popped one in.

I've never watched a porno, but from the looks of it, my wife does. As I watched and the focus of the film became clear, I noticed it was my wife. She was dressed in skimpy clothing that I've never seen her wear. Her makeup was dark and she looked like someone I did not know. There she was getting worked over by one, then two men. The look on her face was pure pleasure. She was doing things that we had never done, not even when we were in love. I was in shock, but I could not stop watching her. As I went through the movies there were scenes of her with women, then men, then women and men, I was astounded, I felt if the blood had drained from my body. Who was this woman?

As I sat there, I was brought back to life by the sun piercing through a small area of the blinds. I had spent all night looking at these videos of my wife and her escapades. She was living a life that I had no idea about, a life that she so well covered up, a life that she kept her smiling like Martha Stewart. I wanted to ravish her body like those men, but a part of me was disgusted. I wanted to be angry, but the satisfaction I was getting while watching my wife with these other men would not allow me to. We both were finding pleasure with other people and from the outside it worked. Now from the inside I know it worked too; we did not bring any of our outside doings to the family. I was relieved; the little guilt that I was feeling vanished. So I won't say anything. I wonder if she knew about my affair with Shelly and choose to also say nothing. I will keep my wife's secret; there is no reason for divorce, no reason to argue over something that means nothing. This is what we have become. This is the life we have chosen for ourselves. I will continue to see Shelly and she can continue to be and do whatever she pleases. Whatever made her happy. There was something about seeing my wife with those men, that had me wanting her. After all, she is my wife.

SARAH GREEN

My name is Sarah Green. I am a mother, wife and a friend to very few. I am married to a wealthy man whom I fell deeply in love with ten years ago. Although I love my husband, I also hate what we have become. Our marriage has taken on a form of its own. He lives his life and I've created mine and financially we come together. Yes, he brought me from a long, long way. A way that I will never go back to. This rags to riches situation is a sad and lonely existence, one that is remedied by small doses of cocaine, prescription marijuana, and pills. A lot of pills.

My husband is a short stalky man that dressed well and walked like he had money. He was not the most attractive, but he could sway you to believe that he was the most handsome man in the room. He had that kind of swag that made you want to know him. It was what made me fall in love with him and out again. But there was a weakness underneath that confidence. I knew that my husband was having an affair. I know he vacations with her. I also know that he spends a lot of our money on her. But what he does not know is that I set the whole thing up. I know that he is a weak man. He only has power in the board room. Everywhere else he is a frail little boy waiting to be rescued by a blow job that's tainted with love. I guess I could be angry, yell and scream because he took the bait, but that would also mean that I do not know my husband and I do. Maybe too well. Shelly keeps my husband busy while I do what I want. With all this money, I do more than just shop. I make full use of my time and body.

To our friends, or rather his friends, we are the perfect family. We did things together that made us look like the perfect family. Oh, how we have come accustomed to these masks. We put our masks on that fit so well, that sometimes we fool ourselves. At times, I actually believe that we are still in love and that we are happy and that this nightmare that we live in is just a small bump in the road to another level of happiness. I want to believe that the fact that I haven't heard him tell me he loves me in over three years is just a figment of my imagination or that the last time we made love I could have sworn he called me Shelly or that every time he is with her he never bothers to even shower before coming home. He brings her Clinique Happy smelling ass in our home. Am I imagining all of this? Of course not, no one could have orchestrated a perfect life.

I had to spice it up, spice my life up, and turn this whole situation into something worth having. I also wanted to punish my husband for being a stiff dick. He paid no attention to the fact that I was his wife, and that I spend more time with the kids than he ever did. I had to punish him my way, blind him with someone else's affection so that I could conceal my own. I had his children because I was bored. I thought he would also be home, but none of that happened. The children spend a lot of time with their nanny, I am sure they are better off. I love my twins, lucky me, but this life has created a void. I have yet to connect to them the way a mother should. Shit, I survived without a mother's love, so with what they are getting they should be fine. I watch them grow like plants and water them when necessary.

I go into mother/wife mode when he walks in the door. He has no idea that I spend most of the day drugged up, a hit here, and a hit there. How else could I function in this world that I know nothing about? When it is time to entertain clients in the east wing of this house, I become another person. I am in control, they need me. They show me their love, but what they pay. He would probably die if he knew that his wife was giving sexual favors to Brian, the Chief Operations Officer, who likes to be tied up and have the shit beat out of him or that Chris in Advertising & Marketing is really gay and likes all kinds of shit up his ass. A man that likes it in the ass as much as he does, has to be a dysfunctional gay and probably should lose his wife. Those are the people that can afford me, those are the people I have access to and those are the people I use. Maybe that's my sickness and they are the cure. I fulfill sexual desires while fulfilling my own in the process. I created this world because my real life is such an incomplete sentence on a blank page. In this life, I can be whomever I want. The doctor, nurse, or Dominate Denise. On any given day at any given moment and there's a part of me that enjoys it all. My husband, my dear husband if only he would catch a clue. He may be rich, but this little venture is making me richer. Sex is my business.

Maybe I should be getting therapy for my sexual libido. But

who would I be bullshitting? Therapy for sex? It's the most natural form of expression; some need it more than others. Is not like alcohol where you can overdo it and go into a coma or drive off the road and kill someone. All it takes is another person or two, or maybe just you. I prefer two or three. I love to have many things done to me all at once. My level of stimulation is very high, so high that I have to get high to catch up with it. But so what? It helps me to maintain this image we have created. This ridiculous lifestyle that we're so proud of, so don't be mad at me.

Although I have often thought of killing my husband, I have not had the time to plan it properly. I know a lot of weak assholes, who would be easy to manipulate and more than willing to do the job. But they are not strong enough to not break if under pressure. So, I leave things as they are. I float through this life on a cloud of uncatchable smoke. I enjoy what I do, I have to. There are not many other things that interest me or keep me occupied like sex does. This therapy thing keeps entering my mind like I have some kind of problem. To pretend they do not exist a place I visit while in REM sleep. It takes another kind of strength to live every day and that is what I am made of. I am just making adjustments to fit my current lifestyle. I hate to think that my husband doesn't love me like he used to. Maybe he does still love me, maybe I should be turning these tricks for him and not his co-workers, but I can't turn back now, I am too far gone. I am obsessed. It had been a late night for me, and an even earlier morning. I was coming from Napa with my "friends", and it had been a very eventful weekend. I was tired, but as my driver came close to my home, I noticed that Stephens car was in the driveway. What was he doing home early? Had his "business trip" not gone well? I wasn't really interested in knowing all the details, but he was home, so I had to pretend like I was happy to see him.

When I entered my home, I could smell that Stephen had been in the shower. The house was filled with new roses and flowers everywhere. What was going on? Had someone died? I looked in the kitchen and there was lunch with my favorite wine, chocolate, and strawberries, had he brought his whore to my fucking home? This man had grown pretty bold, but had he lost his mind too?

I still had not seen him yet and I was wondering what was going on. As I walked up the stairs there was rose petals on the stairway and little notes that said, I love you, I miss you and I want you. Where were the kids and the nanny? I was confused and scared, what was I going to find when I walked into my bedroom. If his whore was in my bed, then they both had crossed the line and I would definitely file for divorce. We never bring our garbage into our home, well not directly.

I walked into the bedroom and there he was on the bed completely naked with nothing but a rose covering his dick. It was my husband in a way that I had not ever seen him. He was smiling when he got up and walked over to me and landed a kiss on me that almost took my breath away. He put his hand around my neck and pushed me against the wall. Kissed me so deep, I was afraid. I dropped my bags and he picked me up and carried me over to the bed and ravished my body. Fucked me so hard from the back, I thought I saw stars. He kissed me all over, he touched me in places that I thought he forgot about. What was bringing all this on? Was he going to kill me later? I could not help but enjoy what was happening. After a moment I could not help but reciprocate what I was being given. We were making love like never before, it was a moment that I must have been starving for. A moment that I thought was completely lost between the two of us. Everything he wanted to say, he said with the motion of him going inside and out of me. And I heard him loud and clear, but what was behind this new found interest in me? What did this mean? There was no way I could confess my wrongdoings. There was no way, I could let him know what kind of business I had been running.

We must have made love for a whole day and night, inside of the bedroom. The nanny had taken the kids and made meals for us. I was feeling happy but needed a pill or two to help me process what was happening. I know there must be something else coming. Was he planning to kill me? Had he found out about my sexual rendezvous? I did not know what to ask or how to respond. So, I will let him lead the way and say nothing.

MR. & MRS. GREEN

My husband was a mad man. He ravished me and I did not even recognize who he was. After all these years of marriage, he had never fucked me the way that he did. I wasn't sure how to feel or where this was coming from. I was lying in bed exhausted looking at him sleep. I was starting to feel guilty for all the shit I was doing. I was selling my body for my pleasure. I was using drugs to get through the day. There were so many things going through my mind that I would have to wait for Stephen to wake up to really know what's going on. I was scared and nervous being he has not said a word to me.

I slipped out the bed into the shower. I wanted to just enjoy a nice hot shower because I was not sure what my husband had in store for me today. I checked on the kids and they were out having breakfast with our nanny. I could just replay in my head all that happened last night and how I have got to this point in my life.

I had always enjoyed sex. I thought it was a natural desire that everyone had. I have been having sex since I was thirteen. I had been enjoying it since I was twenty. That is the only way I know how to connect. I had enjoyed several relationships before I met my husband. There were many times that I thought about being an escort. I loved having sex, so why not get paid for it? I remember being dumped once because my boyfriend thought I was using him for sex. The nerve of a man to dump a woman because of her sex drive. If you couldn't fuck me back to happiness or slay me to sleep, having you in my world would be pointless.

I was taught at a very young age about the power of sex. It can drive a man insane; some have been known to kill for it. Every time I have sex with a man or woman it is my way of controlling them. I know you are going to want more. I know you will be back. I was taught that if you throw sex into the mix, you can negotiate anything.

I had a friend who used to always beg me to eat my pussy. I only thought of him as a friend and I knew that if he crossed that line, our friendship would be at risk. After years of begging, I finally let him eat it for five hundred dollars and only until I came. In essence, you had the control if I came in five minutes or thirty minutes that was up to you, but once I did it, it was over. That was easy money to me and I thought if he would pay that much to just eat it, imagine how much money I could make if I have sex for just fifteen minutes. And that's how it all began. It became a game to me. I felt powerful and in control. I built up my clientele and soon I was being paid up to eight hundred dollars just to lick it.

I thought being married and having children would help facilitate the changes I needed to make to live a normal life. I wanted to have the husband, kids, and the white picket fence. But somewhere in gaining all that I desired in one life, I still had the desires to fulfill in the next. I was not happy with just being a wife and mother. I had to go back to what I knew best and what satisfied me.

I got out the shower after what seemed like hours. I stepped into our bedroom and my husband was sitting on the edge of the bed in his navy-blue robe, with a cup of coffee in his hand.

"Would you like some coffee?", he said.

'Sure, thank you." The energy in the room was thick and intense, I had no idea where this was coming from. He sat there looking at me, while I was looking at him.

"Are you happy?", he asked.

"I am ok."

"What would make you happy right now?"

I did not need this shit, why is he asking me if I am happy? What do you think? I needed to pop some pills or snort some coke. I cannot handle this questioning shit.

"I love you, you are my wife. I spent most of yesterday morning watching you have sex with other men. At first, I was shocked. You have never done half the shit you do with them, with me. Do you love me?"

I was staring at my husband hearing the words come out of his mouth, but not being able to answer his question. He had found out about my extra-curricular activities. I was busted. But I was more concerned because he was not mad. He had the look of compassion on his face. He wanted to find out more about why I was doing what I was doing. If he asked for a divorce, I would understand. Even though I knew of his affair, it could not compare to all the shit I had been doing. I know that my life is about to crumble. It's time to get off this ride and join the fucking circus.

He walked over to me and kissed me on my neck. It was like the kiss of death. I was nervous. He began to remove my robe. I was still wet from the shower. He turned me over and fucked me again. He pulled my hair and slapped my ass, fucking me so hard that I wanted him to stop. He turned me over and kissed me on the mouth sucking all over my body, throwing me all over the bed, having his way with me. He then leaned over me while putting his hand around my neck, and said, 'Suck my dick like you do on video." I was petrified. I wanted him to stop, but he forced his dick into my mouth. Then he said, "I am not going to divorce you or run what you have going on, but you will do whatever I ask, whenever I ask and with whomever I ask.

Love, Lies, & Lust

Amanda Rae Jackson

I married for the love of money. Only a fool would marry for love. For me, love tends to provide a short-term high and fades like a worn sweater. Considering all the married men that I have fucked it seems to ring true for them as well. Everybody eventually wants something else other than what they are getting. Either you go back to what used to, or you dabble in something new, either way, you're getting fucked. I prefer the married male, I seduce the married female and just play with all else that is in between. I am a true vixen by every meaning of the word. To some, I may appear to be a whore, but I could easily change their opinion with one hour and a strong drink. You have to understand that when you have money it forms the opinion of small minds. I could be a whore, but men will still want to sleep with me. The Kardashian effect. I love myself and I love money. If money is the root of all evil, then I am the seed. Lately, with so much that has been given to me, I haven't had to take anything in a long time. Now, my admirers just watch me and wish and hope that they get chosen to be in my presence.

It can sometimes be a task to be wanted all the time, by so many people. I guess the opposite is not being wanted by anyone, which to me is a lot worse. To know that at any given moment if I choose I can have you, no matter who you may think you belong to. It first becomes a thought, then an act, then a moment, then you become part of my past; only to be revisited if I want you to be a part of my future. It was like magic. Even those I don't want wonder why I don't want them. I can make the most confident man or woman feel insecure and make them think twice about how to approach me. Everyone wants to be wanted and sometimes it does not matter by whom. It all comes down to me giving a touch, the desired feeling, providing that temporary feeling of love and meeting that basic human need, or at least what they think they may need. Well, when it comes to me, if I am giving it, then I will also make you believe that you need it, otherwise what's the point?

Amanda Rae Jackson, I heard she was as cold as they come. How I managed to marry a computer whiz is beyond me. He was a small reminder that anything is possible. Maybe it was my fired-up nature packed into this five feet four frame. Or maybe the fact that I am educated, master's degree in psychology. Or maybe I have found my way to work magic among the common, who are ruled by visual stimulation and smoke mirrors. The believable lie. Whatever it may be, it works, or better yet, I make it work.

I married Jeffrey Jackson five years ago. I give him what to think and I show him what to believe. We have no children. He is not the most attractive man that I ever saw, and is quite boring and simple. There is no spark, just plain ole' married love. You know the kind that you just learn to deal with because the money is long and the time spent is short. The kind of marriage that you just been in this too long kind of love, to complain or cause any problems, it is what it is. I wish we had some excitement in our marriage, but it's not like I did not know what I was getting into. And people who say that their mate changes when they get married, no they don't, you just refused to see who they are before you get married. It takes three to six months for someone to truly reveal themselves, if you find additional bad shit after that, then you are the one sleep. Hearing that chick was a whore when she married you or that fool was a woman chaser when he married you, or a liar, wife beater, child molester, drug user or whatever, people rarely change, you either learn to ignore their shit or accept their shit; whatever that shit may be. So I knew my husband would be boring. He gave me a professional fuck every now and then. It didn't matter that he could not perform properly to meet my needs and he was good for "show". Kind of like my own personal husband with major benefits; a nerd even, so I kept him. We dated for 6 months before we were married. I wanted him, not because I loved him, but because I knew that he would take care of me and he loved me. If his simple needs were meet, I was free to do whatever I wanted. Deep inside I knew marriage would not make me a faithful woman. My heart just did not have the capacity to love that way. I do not allow that emotion in my life, it can trick you and I could never submit to it. Every move I have made all of my life has been a meticulous one and one with a purpose. I've never done anything out of the kindness of my heart because there was no kindness in it. I cared enough to not get careless in my decisions, but probably not careful enough not to sleep with my husband's assistant,

Shelly. She had been the exception to my golden rule to never sleep with the help.

Shelly Parks, a slut indeed, but a classy one. When I saw that my husband had hired her without my consent, I was a bit shocked. She was different in a way that I just could not figure out and I can spot a nasty girl a mile away and I knew she would be able to keep a secret. She had a long weave down to her butt, full lips and thighs, you would never suspect her of being a lesbian. I really don't like to know much about the people I conquer, but from what I allowed her to spill she had been adopted, then a run-away, then a stripper, found redemption, went to computer school and is now my husband's assistant. She had a series of failed relationships, then one with a woman that allowed her to not only spread her wings but her legs. A full blown out the closet lesbian and apparently haven't looked back. I loved the wounded. They are the ones that are the easiest to manipulate and control. Again, fulfilling that need to be needed. You can hurt them and then soothe them. I needed her on my team not only to devour me but to serve me and be a spy. She would become my own personal pet.

I guess you may be wondering how I got to this place? How I have such disregard for humans and have this heartless approach to life. I too was a wounded soul, until I took control of my life. I learned early that you can't be too nice and people prefer it when you have a high potential of being a bitch. Even the most church-going, choir singing person has the ability to be a church-going, choir singing bitch, they just turn it off on Sunday's. In this life, you can spend six days a week being a total inconsiderate bitch and on Sunday it can all be erased with a prayer and three hail Mary's. Sounds like a pretty good deal to me.

My father was a Baptist preacher and my mother was a fool. He screwed everyone from the church secretary to the mothers of the church, all in the name of God. He also fathered two children with two different women; women that my mother brought into the church. Yes, she stayed and continued to praise God on the front left pew of the church for many years as if nothing was happening. I guess if you did not acknowledge that something was happening, then it probably really wasn't. Perception is reality, right? She not only lived in denial she created it and rowed in it often in her little canoe. It was a place of comfort for her. Her idea of being strong was not facing anything and going on with life like it was a perfect sunny day. I would have preferred her to show some signs of life, but I guess never facing anything takes a level of strength too. This denial thing is a silent killer and I believe at some point my mother began to die. It was a place that I never wanted to be. Religion and its flaws. Who made all this shit up? The rules and regulations of life? I grew up quick and empty. That's all you need to know; all that other shit in between is really none of your business.

SHELLY PARKS

The road that had me prostituting between San Pablo Ave and the tenderloins was long and hard. I was completely lost. Giving blowjobs on the local doughboys was a very dangerous and lifeless job. When they found out I was really a boy dressed as a girl, my life almost ended. The reality of letting a boy give them blowjobs hit hard, so I was beaten into a coma. I was in the hospital the whole summer. I knew then, I had to change my life.

Even though I have changed a lot, there is so much of my character that I cannot let go; like the hustle in me and my ability to recognize a come up. I love it all and I am not ashamed, but I had to leave Gerald Daniel Parks behind, and bring Ms. Shelly Renee Parks to life.

I was born a boy. I was a skinny boy with a high-pitched voice and even now at twenty-seven, my voice is something that really has not changed much. Along with the hormones and working out with dabs of steroids now and then, I was transformed into a voluptuous woman. At five feet ten, I could not be missed. I had always been fair skinned due to my interracial background. My mother was white of Irish blood and my father was Mexican and Black, so I was a mutt, like most of America. I was fucked up, I was confused and I had been abandoned. And once I decided to become a woman, I was not looking back. I wanted breasts and a pussy and smooth skin. All I needed was someone to pay for it all.

It was time for my full sex change, I had already acquired some 38C's so that part had already been taken care of. When I found a trick to finance changing my sexual organs, it was like my prayers had been answered. I had arranged a meeting with a woman through my escort service. Although I do not usually sex up women, this particular woman had a special request and wanted me to meet her in person. When she spoke on the phone, her voice was deep and raspy, like she smoked chimneys. That was the beginning of my relationship with her husband, the suave and intelligent businessman Stephan Green. She basically wanted me to keep her husband company. She wanted me to be a distraction. I would play coy and just give him blow jobs until I was able to get a sex change. He will never know that underneath it all, I was born a man. I had to keep this a secret like my life depended on it.

Stephan gave me whatever I wanted, so when I asked for bigger breasts and a few other things, he easily forked over the money and it was done. I could never let him know the life I had before. Why would he care if what we have makes him so happy? I cared for him a little bit because his wife was such a bitch. I could not get too deep with clients, but Stephan was special, he was really looking for real love. He pretended to have found it with me. Although I was purchased by his wife, I could never let him know the truth or get too involved. I am not giving up anything for nothing, I am financially secure but emotionally bankrupt, and the price was high for this short-lived life. He was my only client, I had to find something else to do with my life before I get too attached.

I've always been an attractive boy, but I am an irresistible woman. This body was given to me by the surgeon gods. I added what I needed and will remove what I no longer wanted. When I am finally able to have sex as a woman Stephen would be my first. He should be more than happy to be getting more than just a blowjob and a blowing on the ass. Once I have a vagina, my journey will be complete and I could fully live my life.

My other life consisted of my everyday job of being an Executive Assistant. Being an escort provided certain benefits, but I did not want to do that shit forever. The first thing I did as a girl was got a degree in computer science. Shortly after, I landed a computer assistant job working for the most amazing and intelligent man I have ever seen. A little short for my taste, but I was curious about him from the moment I saw him. I only dreamed that he felt the same way about me because he was married. If his wife got one snippet of an idea that I wanted her husband, she would seek me out and devour me like a tiger eating raw meat. She wanted me all to herself and I was, kind of. She is a strange little freak with weird taste and fetishes, but so was I, which made it easy for me to accommodate. How the fuck did I get to go from a man to a woman to be in a lesbian relationship? Mi vida loca!

Amanda Rae Jackson was not a bitch to be reckoned with. She controlled so much of her husband's life, it was like she was living a second life through him. I am not sure if there was any love on her part. If there was love, it must have been hidden in a small part behind her cold heart. She never asked for anything, but demanded it from anyone that crossed her path. I guess that is how I became involved with her. I have never been attracted to women, even as a boy, but this woman's aura was intoxicating. She seemed like a small woman, with long legs, she always wore mini-skirts and 5-inch heels, so I never knew how tall the bitch really was. Her makeup was always flawless like she stopped by the MAC counter every morning before work. She managed to bring out her hazel eyes on her dark mocha skin. The bitch was stunning! What a fierce piece of fish! Her shoulder length hair framed her face and made her look younger than her years. Her clothes always fit her well. She didn't seem like a label whore, but she wore the best. She dressed for the office every day, although this bitch did not have a job whatsoever. She had a walk that said she meant business and an attitude that said, "Please don't fuck with me because if you look at me, I will medusa yo' ass into stone". Respect that shit or get out the fuckin' way.

She fed you, nurtured you, and then she raped you with her undeniable lust for whatever it was she wanted; from me she wanted sex. She wanted to touch my breasts and talk to me, she wanted to lick me all over and do things that made me ill. Again, I was being abused, but I felt sorry for her. I felt like I needed to do this for her or she would make my life and Jeffrey's life miserable. Jeffrey did not deserve that.

She wanted to know my life story, so I made up one. If she

knew what the real story was, she had the power to eliminate me from the face of the earth. Although she never gave me any indication of her being a violent person, that was the main reason I was afraid of her. She could kill you in silence and then get up and have a cup of coffee or tea for breakfast. I hated her and admired her in a strange way all at the same time. I wanted to kill her and protect her. By her, I was amused and I felt owned by my situation.

She came into the office maybe once or twice a week. I think there may have been a certain level of guilt of cheating on her husband that she carried, but never showed. She came in to check on her husband. She didn't act like she loved him, but she protected her investment like Fort Knox. When she came into the office everyone would just get all their P & Q's in order and have everything all nice and neat. She was known to rip your head off or fire you on the spot if she didn't like what she was seeing. She had a lot of power for someone who did not work for her husband's company. I wanted to tell her, "Don't worry Ms. Jackson, I am watching your husband and one day he will be mine." That was my plan and with this heartless bitch you had to be ten steps ahead and plan carefully. But shit, who was I foolin'? This bitch could have me chopped up and mailed to a third world country before I could even formulate the thought to steal her husband. I shall obey and play nice, for now.

It was cold and rainy when she invited me over to talk. Usually, she wanted to meet me in a secluded hotel, but this time she wanted me to meet her in her office. No one had ever seen the inside of her office and lived to tell about it. It was located at the top of the Tribune building in downtown Oakland. Her husband's business had occupied at least 3 of the floors, but the top one belonged to her. I was nervous as hell. What did she want? Had she somehow found out I was interested in her husband? I prolonged the meeting by saying there were things I needed to finish, but she insisted that I come right now.

There she was sitting in her office chair in an office that looked more like a vault. Everything was dark with a small light on her cherry wood desk. There were plaques on the wall, not sure of what, maybe they were her degree's or her certificates that certified her as a crazy bitch. There were pictures of her and Jeffrey. Pictures that showed their love of traveling, their marriage photo and a few people that I had never seen before. She asked me to take a seat. I was sweating, my weave was itching and I needed a drink. I wanted to run out of there, but I sat down and pretended everything was normal. Considering that she was a bitch that got to the point, this seemed like it would not be a drawn-out meeting.

"Hello, Shelly, how are you today? She asked, looking directly in my eyes and never moving them to any other part of my being. I was frozen. My heart was beating faster than I could stand.

"I am fine, Mrs. Jackson, how are you?"

"Better than most", she replied, as she smiled as if she knew something I didn't. Then there was this silence that seems to last forever. I tried to not look in her eyes, but once I did, then the shit came.

"You want my husband"? She asked.

"Want your husband? No, of course not. Mr. Jackson loves you, everyone knows that".

Yes, everyone does know that, except you.

My heart dropped in my lap. What was this crazy bitch talking about? Had she found out about our affair? Yes, I was sleeping with them both, one out of necessity and the other out of pleasure. But as sure as my name was Shelly Renee Parks, I was not going to admit anything. She would have to kill me first, and from the looks of it, that's probably what she had in mind.

"Mrs. Jackson, there is nothing going on between me and your husband, I would be a fool to jeopardize my j…she interrupted.

"Yes, you would be and you are. Stop lying to me, you are making me sick." She starts to laugh, "You really thought you could fuck me and my husband and have me not find out? You must be proud that you now have a pussy as opposed to a dick now. Yes, bitch I know who you are. I mean, I know who you really are. Gerald! The little faggot from the tenderloin who has done well by being a high-class call girl. You see honey, I have friends in high places and I know you have Mr. Stephen Green going out of his mind thinking he's all in love and shit and that's all fine and dandy, but you, my dear, have fucked with the wrong husband.

I was shocked, stunned even. I had no words of denial anymore. My composure had completely been exposed. I was shaking at the thought of what this crazy bitch would do to me. I just sat there waiting for her to kill me. We were in this office that was dark and secluded, with just me and her. No one would know. Who would look for me? My past did not know Shelly Parks. I sat there in disbelief, listening to her rant. She did not seem pissed but amused by the fact that her husband had the nerve to have an affair.

As she walked around the room thinking and planning, this is what she demanded of me. She wanted to prepare to divorce her husband and have him mysteriously die in the process. She wanted to take everything he had, including the company, and she wanted me to continue to fuck her husband and record every session. She wanted everything we did on tape, our conversations, our hotel reservations, everything.

She looked at me as if she dared me to say no. I was afraid and also glad to have my life. How could I do this? She was cheating too. I agreed, as she kissed me on the mouth and slowly pulled up my skirt and fingered me. She looked me in my eyes the whole time, daring me to deny her or move.

"Nice work, but don't play with me bitch. Next time it will be your life".

As soon as I left our meeting, I called Jeffrey. He did not answer, so he must be with Amanda. I was frozen. I could not set Jeffrey up for failure, I had to figure this out. She was trying to tear him down and get ownership of his company and I was not going to have any parts of it. I loved him and I had to let him know her plans. How did she know about Sarah? This evil bitch had to be stopped.

I haven't seen Stephan for many weeks. After our trip to the Virgin Islands, we didn't see each at all. I was concerned because there was a chance that I would not be receiving my three-thousand dollars a month anymore. And if Sarah knows Amanda, soon all this shit will be over. Sarah had already told Amanda about my sex change, soon Jeffrey would know. Maybe I should just tell him that I was born a male, his wife is trying to kill him and let's go away together. He probably would not believe me and there was a chance that once he hears that I was born a male that it will be over between us. If I was serious about him and wanted him in my life, I had, to be honest. I had to reveal everything and see what happens. I didn't like being deceived and I should have told him by now.

It was passed midnight when my phone rang.

"Hello?"

"Shelly, it's Jeff, are you ok?

"Yes, are you?"

"Yeah, Amanda has lost her mind. She knows about us and she wants to talk to the both of us."

"The both of us?"

"Yes, the both of us."

Why the fuck did she want to talk to the both of us? My mind was racing; I was not sure what she had on her mind. She was a crazy bitch so this could go really great or really bad. I ended the call and told Jeffry I would see him at work.

It was 5:30 a.m. I received a text from Amanda telling me to be at the W Hotel in San Francisco at 8 p.m. When she wanted me we would always meet somewhere outside the city, but this was right downtown. I wasn't sure. I got dressed in my sexiest black dress. I wore five-inch heels and made sure my weave was on tight. I had no idea what the day had in store and I wanted to look as fierce as any bitch could. I went in to work like it was a regular day. Jeffrey was not here yet. He usually would send me a good morning text, but this morning I did not hear from him. I wanted to let him know about Amanda's plans, but I'll wait until he comes in for work.

It was eleven a.m. and Jeffrey was still not at work. I was starting to get concerned because he never missed work. It was the end of the day and I still had not heard from him. I left work and went to a local bar to drink before I had to be at the W Hotel. I sat there wondering what this bitch was up to. I had enough money to not show up and leave the state, but what would happen to Jeffrey. I needed to stay and make sure that he was ok. He is my future. Hopefully, Amanda has fucked up enough to make him realize that she doesn't love him.

It was getting close to the time to be at the hotel. I had thought of every scenario possible. What did this bitch have up her sleeve? I still had not heard from Jeffrey since he told me about the meeting. I was worried, but I am going to continue to throw down these Tokyo Tea's until I can no longer feel anything.

It was seven forty-five, it was time to head to the hotel. Once I arrived, I received a text from Amanda that said, Come to room 3300. The thirty-third floor was a long ride. I knocked on the door and once it was opened I saw Jeffrey naked and tied up to the bed. He looked unconscious but I could not tell exactly because the room was dark with just a slim of light coming in from the city lights, and I still didn't see Amanda.

Then a voice from the bathroom said, "Since I don't trust

you to do what I asked, I wanted to make sure you did what I said. Take your clothes off, and let the show begin." Amanda was making her way out the bathroom to the couch, she was holding a video camera and smoking o a joint. Did she want to video me and Jeffrey having sex? She was getting desperate and I was not going to be having sex with her husband on camera. She must be out of her mind. When I was finally able to see her, she looked deranged. She was dressed in a casual sweat suit; way below her standard for clothes. He hair was pulled back in a bun and she had on almost no make-up. I had to find a way to reason with this crazy bitch.

"Amanda, what are you doing, are you sure you want this?"

"Yes, I want you to fuck my husband since he likes transgender ass bitches. Y'all getting' more and more popular these days, but not with mine!" I want to see him enjoy a man that is now a woman, who in a few minutes won't be on this fucking earth anymore, so who gives a fuck? Who are you going to call? Who can you tell bitch? Her deep laughter made me realize that she was enjoying all of this. I was speechless. I wish I would have taken that flight to somewhere else.

"I can't fuck your husband, Amanda."

"Why not, don't you love him? Wasn't it your plan to run away with my husband?"

"No...." Then the gun came out. She was aiming it at my head. I looked at her and she was serious. I was scared and not sure how to get out of this. I refused to fuck her husband. I was trying to buy time by talking to her, but this gun had me feeling like I was running out of time. I closed my eyes and if she wanted to shoot me, she could. I no longer cared about her and what she would do to me. It was time I took a chance.

Amanda was high and getting hysterical she was twirling that gun around like it was a baton. I was waiting for her to turn her back. Just as I thought to tackle her she begins to turn around, yelling and screaming about being the baddest bitch and how she runs the world. I rushed her to the floor, the gun went flying in the air. Before I knew it, I was all on top of her beating her in the face. It was almost like I could not stop, but I did once I realized she wasn't moving. I grabbed the phone and called nine-one-one.

Six months had passed and I had moved on with my life. I had the chance to go away and travel for a few months, I really had to clear my head. So much had happened in such a short time. With all that I had been through in my life, this was the icing on the cake but it was nothing that I couldn't handle. I promised myself that once this was all over I was moving out of California. I wanted to get more plastic surgery and really start fresh; but first I had to stay around for the trial of Amanda Ray Jackson for the murder of her husband, Jeffrey Jackson.

To be continued....

ABOUT THE AUTHOR:

L.L. Walton, the author of *Please Don't Date Me-100 Reasons Why*, is currently living in Oakland, California. Her interest range from writing about everyday life to the perils of love and relationships.

You can enjoy her writing skills at http://lavidus.blogspot.com, where you also have access to some of her most popular blogs.

Please stay tuned for the release of ***Please Don't Date Me-100 Reasons Why*** Volume II & III.

You can follow her on twitter @LLWriter or on Facebook at https://www.facebook.com/llwriter

AND DON'T FOR GET TO LOOK FOR MY 1ST BOOK THAT WILL SURELY HELP YOU AVOID THE PITFALLS OF DATING...